"Look at you...
bedraggled, wet to the skin!"

"I couldn't sit by while everyone else worked to save the harvest." Camille flung the words at him. "Besides, I didn't think you'd hear about it."

"Hear about it.... It's the talk of the valley!"

"Blame it on my barbaric American upbringing," Camille retorted.

Suddenly Antoine laughed, and his gaze softened. *"Mon Dieu,* you are a lovely handful." Gently, he traced the outline of her lips with his fingertips. "You could drive a man crazy."

Camille hoped she wouldn't betray her agonizing love for him.

"If I give in gracefully, at least I can keep tabs on you." Antoine shook his head in exasperation. "I'll tell Remi to let you work."

As Camille watched him leave, she wondered why she didn't feel like celebrating. After all, she had just won the war.

WELCOME
TO THE WONDERFUL WORLD
OF *Harlequin Romances*

Interesting, informative and entertaining,
each Harlequin Romance portrays an appealing
and original love story. With a varied array
of settings, we may lure you on an African safari,
to a quaint Welsh village, or an exotic Riviera
location—anywhere and everywhere that adventurous
men and women fall in love.

As publishers of Harlequin Romances, we're
extremely proud of our books. Since 1949,
Harlequin Enterprises has built its publishing
reputation on the solid base of quality and
originality. Our stories are the most popular
paperback romances sold in North America; every
month, six new titles are released and sold at
nearly every book-selling store in Canada and the
United States.

For a list of all titles currently available,
send your name and address to:

HARLEQUIN READER SERVICE,
(In the U.S.) P.O. Box 52040, Phoenix, AZ 85072-2040
(In Canada) P.O. Box 2800, Postal Station A
5170 Yonge Street, Willowdale, Ont. M2N 5T5

We sincerely hope you enjoy reading
this Harlequin Romance.

Yours truly,

THE PUBLISHERS
Harlequin Romances

Château Villon

Emily Spenser

Harlequin Books

TORONTO • NEW YORK • LONDON
AMSTERDAM • PARIS • SYDNEY • HAMBURG
STOCKHOLM • ATHENS • TOKYO • MILAN

Original hardcover edition published in 1984
by Mills & Boon Limited

ISBN 0-373-02668-4

Harlequin Romance first edition January 1985

Printed in U.S.A.

CHAPTER ONE

'Darn!' Camille exclaimed as the strap of her bag broke. She had been fishing for change to tip the porter, who waited impatiently near her two suitcases.

It was almost the last straw. She was tired and grubby from the overnight transatlantic flight and the train trip from Paris to Dijon. And already she was homesick for the Napa Valley, Dad and Bernie. They had told her she would be met by a distant cousin, but all the passengers had dispersed and she was alone on the platform with a very aggrieved-looking porter.

With relief, she found a few francs. She had been sure she had dropped them there when she had landed at Orly. So intently had she been searching that she didn't notice a tall man approach from behind her, until he dismissed the suddenly very respectful porter with a large tip and a brief *merci*.

Camille turned and found herself staring up at a pair of deep brown eyes. He was by far the most handsome man she had ever seen, with dark hair, classical features and an incredible bronze tan. She was impressed by his height and the width of his shoulders, but most of all she was struck by the aura of money and power that somehow radiated from him. His mouth, firm but sensual, was smiling sardonically as he studied her.

'You must be my cousin Miss Fouquet, no?' he said in English.

There was a clear note of disdain in his voice as he said the word *cousin*, and she was suddenly conscious of her rumpled, inexpensive dress and the wisps of hair escaping from the unaccustomed knot at the nape of her neck. She had no intention, though, of letting this arrogant, disquietingly handsome man sense her discomfort. 'Yes, I am Camille Fouquet,' she said, holding herself straight.

'Welcome to France, Miss Fouquet. I am Antoine Jules de Breze. I hope that you enjoy your stay and that it will be a productive one,' he said, with one eyebrow raised mockingly. Inexplicably, hostility smouldered in his dark eyes.

She raised her chin and spoke coolly, 'I'm sure I shall, although at the present I'm tired and should appreciate it if you would take me to see my grandfather as soon as possible.' Camille hoped she sounded more nonchalant than she felt. Clearly, her cousin knew she was here to try to get a loan from her grandfather, and he disapproved. She was terribly embarrassed, and, if it weren't for Dad and Bernie counting on her, she would have slapped that mocking look off his arrogant face and headed straight back to the airport.

'Of course.' Antoine bowed sarcastically to her. 'Follow me, please.' He spoke abruptly to a middle-aged, uniformed man standing deferentially nearby: 'Pierre, take these bags to the car.' As an afterthought, he said to Camille, 'Your grandfather's chauffeur.'

The man approached them and, to Camille's surprise, respectfully touched his cap in salute to her.

Then he picked up her scuffed, inexpensive luggage, and waited for them to follow him through the station.

Seething with indignation, Camille longed to tell Antoine de Breze exactly what she thought of him and his manners in some very explicit French terms, but she wasn't about to volunteer anything about herself to this infuriating man, especially that she had been brought up bilingually and her French was better than his English. Never in her life had she developed so instant and deep a dislike for anyone. She couldn't help but notice, however, how attractive he was to other women. As they walked through the crowd, the elegantly dressed Antoine drew their glances like a magnet, and she must have looked like a drab sparrow beside him.

Outside the station a long, black limousine was parked on the narrow, cobble-stoned street. Camille's eyes widened; she was barely able to restrain her gasp of surprise. She had known her grandfather was well off, but she hadn't any idea he was wealthy.

Pierre opened the trunk to deposit her bags while Antoine opened the back door and helped a striking young woman out. The woman tossed aside a fashion magazine when she emerged, and placed an impeccably manicured hand lightly, but possessively, on Antoine's arm.

'Miss Camille Fouquet, may I introduce Miss Eugénie Jusserand?' he said in polite tones, the mockery absent from his tone for once.

'*Enchantée*,' Eugénie drawled, obviously anything but enchanted. With her sleek, dark hair swept up in smooth waves, she looked as if she had just stepped out of the magazine she had been reading. Her face was flawlessly made up and her pale-blue eyeshadow matched the blue silk dress that clung to her elegant figure.

'It's nice to meet you,' answered Camille in English, knowing she didn't sound too gracious herself.

'Eugénie and her brother are old family friends who are visiting from Lyon,' said Antoine, helping Camille into the car. As he turned to assist Eugénie, he murmured something to her. Inadvertently, Camille heard Eugénie reply in French:

'What do you expect from a girl whose mother was a peasant?'

Camille blushed, and her eyes filled with tears. She turned her head as if to look out the window when Eugénie got in. She was mortified and bewildered, although she knew that the rude remark had not been intended for her ears. Why were they treating her this way? How could she have offended these rich, self-assured people from another world? Was it the loan? How much could that matter to them? This car alone must cost twice what she would ask of her grandfather. With an effort she kept back her tears, but her throat was tight with the strain.

No, she thought, looking out of the window, seeing nothing, it wasn't the loan. It was the fact that her mother had been a maid in her grandfather's house. This, Camille had learned years ago. With a child's thoughtless persistence, she had wormed out of her father the romantic story he had never before hinted at, and to which he never again referred.

Her grandfather had ruthlessly cut off his only son without a franc when Jean Adrien had insisted on marrying the beautiful servant girl with whom he was hopelessly in love. The young man, hurt and angry, had left at once for America with his bride . . . and with his friend Bernard Fouquet, her grandfather's master vintner, who had resigned in disgust over the incident. How Bernie managed to get the old man to let him take three bags of cuttings from the estate's vines, Jean Adrien had never learned.

From those cuttings had come the modest Fouquet Vineyard in California. And from Bernie had come Camille Fouquet's name, for Jean Adrien had discarded his own surname and adopted Bernie's. He had done it, he told her, out of affection and respect for his old friend. He had also done it, Camille knew without being told, to emphasise his alienation from his own family. He wanted no ties to those who had spurned his beloved Marie.

Lost in her thoughts, Camille stared out of the car window, responding only in monosyllables to Antoine's half-hearted attempts at conversation. Eventually he shrugged and gave up, while Eugénie read her magazine, managing to appear absorbed and bored at the same time. Camille didn't trust herself to speak, afraid she would either cry, tell them off, or do both. And, sick at heart as she was, she wasn't going to do anything that might keep her from accomplishing her mission.

She soothed herself with thoughts of home, and promised herself that once there, she would work her fingers to the bone to help pay back every cent with interest. Gradually, with the resilience of youth, Camille began to forget about the other occupants of the car and to marvel at the scenes unfolding outside the car window. They had left the city behind and were driving through a valley which reminded her powerfully of her own beautiful Napa Valley. Long, low, undulating hills graced with vineyards, lined the road. The vines flowed everywhere, like the sea, spilling around houses and into gardens. Turreted, golden-hued châteaux on the hillsides gave the scene an unreal, fairy-tale-like quality.

This was the famed Côte-d'Or, she realised, turning towards her companions in her excitement. At her movement, Eugénie raised a languid, listless eyebrow. Camille turned again to the window. Soon she began to see signs proclaiming the names of the vineyards: Gevrey-Chambertin, Clos-Vougeot, Nuits-St-Georges, Pommard, Meursault. Her heart pounded with excitement; these were names she had heard since she was a little girl, spoken of with reverence and devotion by the vintners of the Napa Valley.

Even more exciting was the knowledge that she would soon see her own family's ancestral winery. Her father and Bernie had been frustratingly closed-mouthed about its name, saying she'd find out soon enough. Were they silly enough to think she would be disappointed because she had never heard of it? Or because it was outside a well-known wine district? She had only been able to get her grandfather's name, Charles Jean Deslandes, from them because she pointed out she wouldn't even know whom to call if no one met her. She had never heard of a winery named Deslandes, but that didn't mean anything. Frequently wineries were not named after the owning families, or they changed hands many times during their centuries-long histories. In any event, the Deslandes were successful vintners, if one could judge by the car.

Pierre slowed, then turned the big automobile down a narrow lane lined with low stone walls. As far as Camille could tell, they were still in the Côte-d'Or. Could her grandfather own a winery *here*? No, impossible. Dad couldn't possibly have kept such a secret all these years. Perhaps Pierre was taking a short cut out of the valley.

At the sight of a simple, black-lettered sign with a single word—Villon—she temporarily stopped speculating. Wait until she told her friends back home she had seen the famed Villon Vineyards, and even cut across a corner of the estate. It was here, in these fields, that the finest burgundies in the world were unquestionably produced, although experts claimed the wines had declined in the last fifteen years. The vineyard ran up the gently sloping hill almost to the crest. Camille tried to focus on the nearest clusters of grapes as the car sped by. They were plump and already starting to turn purple, but disappointingly similar to the ones Dad and Bernie grew at home.

Half a mile beyond the sign, a lane meandered up the hillside towards a small but elegant château. Camille blinked incredulously as Pierre again slowed and turned up the lane. At the crest of the hill, splendid gilded railings separated the vineyard from the beautifully landscaped formal gardens that surrounded the château. Pierre drove through an ornate, gilded ironwork gate, followed a curving gravel path through the garden and finally stopped, with a crunch of tyres on gravel, in front of the château itself.

It wasn't so small after all, Camille saw, looking with awe at the classical seventeenth-century façade, honey-coloured in the afternoon sun, that rose three storeys to a steeply pitched slate roof. Fortunately, Antoine was giving Pierre instructions about the car, and Eugénie was checking her make-up, so neither noticed the shock on Camille's face. It seemed impossible; the great Villon Winery! So many answers to questions about her father's past clicked into place: his looks—so worn and dispirited lately, but unmistakably aristocratic—his carriage, his reluctance to discuss his past. How much he must have loved his beautiful servant-girl wife to have given this up.

'Miss Fouquet!' Antoine's mocking voice pierced her thoughts.

Camille started, her reflections so intense that she hadn't noticed him impatiently holding the door open and staring down at her. She blushed, knowing that he was thinking how out of place she looked in this environment. As she got out of the car she caught a glance from Pierre. She smiled tentatively, and he returned it with fatherly warmth. He must have known and liked my father, she thought. The idea steadied her.

Eugénie and Antoine barely gave her a glance as they walked up a broad staircase towards a framed and intricately carved doorway where a distinguished, elderly couple awaited them. For the first time in her life Camille was literally tongue-tied. She had planned to greet her grandfather in classical, courteous French, but now even English fled from her mind. She finally found her wits and opened her mouth to speak, but fortunately Antoine cut her off.

'Miss Fouquet, this is Henri, our butler,' he said carelessly.

She was so unnerved at her near-*faux pas*, that she

could only nod at Henri and the plump matronly-looking woman who was introduced as Madame Gounod, the housekeeper.

'Welcome to Château Villon, miss,' they said together in barely understandable English, while Madame Gounod curtsied and Henri offered a sedate half-bow. There was a ready friendliness on their faces, and the knot in Camille's stomach relaxed a little.

'Joséphine!' Antoine called, beckoning to a young, rather plain maid with dark hair, who had been waiting near the bottom of the staircase at the end of a huge entry hall. He turned to Camille. 'Joséphine will be your maid while you are at Château Villon. She is entirely at your disposal.'

After the surprises of the last few minutes, Camille was beyond fazing, and she nodded to Joséphine in what she hoped was a properly ladylike manner.

Antoine addressed the maid in French. 'Miss Fouquet is tired. I'm sure she would like to be shown to her room.' Again he spoke to Camille. 'As I'm sure you know, your grandfather is not a well man. I'll send word to you by Joséphine if he cares to receive you before dinner. We dine at eight o'clock.' He spun on his heel and strode back out of the door.

With a girlish curtsy, Joséphine smiled timidly at Camille and beckoned her to follow her up the marble staircase. Camille was surprised when Joséphine stopped at the first landing and turned down the hall. She had half expected to be shown to some servant's cubbyhole high in the upper reaches of the château. Instead, Josephine opened the door to a magnificent suite: a sitting room furnished with French provincial furniture and tapestries, a large, ornate bath with a marble tub and gilded fixtures, and an airy, pleasant bedroom. Joséphine clearly enjoyed Camille's gasp of pleasure when she opened the French doors and stepped on to a spacious balcony that overlooked the entire, lovely Côte d'Or.

'Do you speak French, miss?' asked Joséphine in halting English.

'Yes, I do,' answered Camille in French. She might as well admit it; she would have to sooner or later, anyway.

Delighted, Joséphine let loose a flood of French. 'We, that is to say, the servants, are so happy to have you here, *mademoiselle*. I myself am too young to have known your father, but my mother, she remembers him well.' Her plain, open face was alight. 'He was truly kind, my mother says, and well-liked. And your mother, they say she was so beautiful! She was my own mother's best friend—' Josephine's cheeks blushed deep red and her hands flew to her mouth in sudden consternation. 'Oh, *mademoiselle*, forgive me, I only meant—'

Camille touched her arm gently. 'There isn't anything to forgive. My mother *was* very beautiful, and my father loved her very much. I hope you'll introduce me to your mother soon. It will be a privilege to meet my mother's closest friend.'

She wasn't at all sure if that was the way to speak to one's personal maid, but the gratitude and devotion that leaped to Joséphine's eyes warmed her heart. Still, some inborn, aristocratic instinct told Camille some distance was necessary. 'I think I might have a bath, now,' she said, 'and get out of these clothes.'

'Of course, *mademoiselle*, I'll bring you some tea,

too. You must be tired.' Joséphine smiled shyly, curtsied, and left, closing the door quietly behind her.

Left alone, Camille explored the rooms, a little intimidated by their grandeur. Her two battered old suitcases, standing dolefully in a corner by the door, contributed the only jarring note to an otherwise ornate, lushly perfect setting.

She opened the suitcases on the parquet floor, afraid to put them on the pristine white silk of the bedspread. She hung her four modest dresses in an immense, dark wardrobe, then stepped back and almost laughed. They looked as forlorn as she felt. Her plain underwear only took up one corner of a drawer in a huge carved chest, and now she understood why her father had wanted her to do some quick shopping for clothes. She had refused, pointing out that they really didn't have the time; they barely had time to borrow the suitcases and arrange for her tickets. He must have given in so easily, Camille realised now, because he'd known it wouldn't really have made any difference. Where would the money have come from to buy clothes that would have fit in at Château Villon?

The second suitcase was full of her casual work clothes: jeans, T-shirts, sweatshirts, and shoes. She smiled to think of the look on Eugénie's face if she ever walked out in her grubbies, as her dad called them.

In the bathroom, she stripped off her clothes and took the clips out of her hair. The long, blonde tresses cascaded down her back. While the tub was filling, she caught a glimpse of her reflection in the gold-framed mirror. She had always had too many important things to do to bother about her looks, but she knew she had possibilities. More than one awkward young man had made that quite clear. Not that any of them had interested her. Indeed, she thought regretfully, she was nineteen, soon to be twenty, and no male had yet created the slightest romantic stirrings in her, let alone evoked the weak-kneed feeling she had read about so often.

She examined the firm-breasted, long-legged girl who stared back at her with green, gold-flecked eyes. There certainly wasn't anything wrong with her, but she could do with some make-up to highlight those eyes, and some colour on her cheeks and lips. She wondered idly what Antoine would think of her, then blushed and stepped rapidly into the bath. Really! What made that thought pop into her mind? She wouldn't give that arrogant snob the time of day much less . . . What a thought!

The tub was so big Camille could stretch out full length. It was black, veined marble, and she was sure the fixtures were real gold. She tried to picture what her father's early life must have been like at Château Villon—certainly far richer than anything she had imagined. How different from his life at the Fouquet Vineyard—especially in the hard years after he and Bernie had first come to America.

With Bernie's savings of three decades they had bought a small plot of land in the Napa Valley. It had taken seven years of back-breaking work to turn those few bags of cuttings into the Fouquet Vineyard, which now produced some of the best Burgundy grapes in the valley. Grapes, but not wine. Because they never managed to acquire the huge amount of capital needed to start their own winery, they had been forced all these years to sell their treasured grapes to the Moran Winery.

Then, just a week ago, had come the day that turned Camille's world topsy-turvy. The scene was burned into her mind. It had been an unusually hot afternoon for August, and she had gone into the house for a glass of water. She had entered the kitchen by the rear door and seen her father slouched over the kitchen table, his back to her. Her heart had constricted with worry. In his middle fifties, Jean Adrien was still a strikingly handsome man, but the proud, erect posture that had always characterised him had deserted him lately. His shoulders seemed always bent, his face tired and drawn.

'Hi, Dad,' she said, as brightly as she could. 'Who's the letter from?'

Evading Camille's eyes, Jean Adrien folded the letter he had been reading, and placed it in his shirt pocket. 'From my father. I wrote to him.'

She stared at him in shock. 'But why?'

'The Moran brothers have sold out to IMBEC Corporation. The deal just went through. Jules warned me about it months ago.'

'Oh, no!' Camille was aghast. For years the big corporations had been slowly moving into the valley, offering enormous sums for the family-owned wineries. Although some owners had sold out, many resisted enticing offers because of their sheer love of winemaking as a way of life. Every time one family sold, it was a tragedy for those that remained, making it more difficult for them to hold on.

Camille was wrenched by a sudden fear. 'IMBEC will buy our grapes, won't they?'

'No,' Jean Adrien said, staring at the table. Then

he finally looked up at her with dull, anguished eyes and a face as grey as slate. He shook his head slowly back and forth. 'No,' he said again, 'they won't.'

Camille longed to throw her arms around the bowed, blue-shirted shoulders, but some dawning, grown-up instinct held her back. She stood still, looking into his tired eyes, painfully aware of how he had aged. He smiled wearily.

'They won't take our grapes,' he said, 'but they've offered to buy us out.'

Camille was stunned. 'Buy us out!' she said incredulously. 'But—'

'At a very decent price,' he added with a bitter smile that cut through her like a knife.

'Oh, Dad,' she said, 'can't we sell our grapes to another winery?'

'No, honey, it's too late to get another contract this year. And if we can't sell our crop we won't have the money to get through until next harvest.' Coming alive, Jean rammed his fist against the table, rose suddenly, and strode agitatedly around the room. 'I won't let them push us out!' He came back to the table and sank into his chair again. 'Even though it means crawling to my damn father for the money to hold on,' he murmured in tightly controlled tones.

'Your father?' Camille could hardly believe it. 'But, Dad, wouldn't it be better to sell? We could start a new vineyard—maybe in Oregon—with the money, couldn't we?' She forced herself to brighten. 'A bigger one, even. I'd rather see us do that, than deal with—' her voice thickened with emotion '—people who tossed you and Mom out just because you loved each other.'

Her father looked stricken. 'I couldn't do that to

Bernie, Camille. He left a part of himself behind when he left France for me, but at least he's still tending vines from the same stock that his father and his father's father tended. Even if they are growing in America.' Jean's hand, lying limp on the scarred table, clenched into a fist. 'And I couldn't'—his voice came near breaking—'I couldn't leave this valley.'

Camille lowered her eyes. She could see her words had hurt her father dreadfully. As usual, she had spoken too quickly, without thinking. Without thinking of Bernie, or of the grave on the hillside above the vineyard, graced always with fresh-cut flowers. She had only been thinking of her own pride, and tears of shame ran suddenly down her cheeks.

Jean Adrien rose quickly and put his arms around her. 'Hey, *ma chérie*, don't cry.'

'I'm so sorry, Dad,' she said, hugging him fiercely. 'I wasn't thinking. Forgive me.'

'Don't worry,' he said, warmly returning her embrace. 'Everything will work out.' He released her and patted the letter in his shirt pocket. 'My father is considering lending us the money, and if he does, maybe we can pay him back in just one season.' He took out a handkerchief and gently brushed away her tears. 'But, you know, he's a very old man now, and he has some quirks. He insists on seeing his grand-daughter before he makes up his mind.'

With thumb and forefinger, Jean Adrien tilted Camille's chin up so that he could look into her face. 'Now dry your tears, pretty one, or those beautiful green eyes will be all red and swollen. *Mon père* is a true Frenchman, very susceptible to a beautiful woman.'

Camille's eyes opened wide. 'Is he coming here?' she asked, with childish, innocent surprise that lightened her father's heart.

He gave a shout of laughter, picturing his proud, aristocratic father sitting down at the plain old kitchen table. 'Not likely. But you're about to leave for France.'

The sound of a door opening in the room next to her jolted Camille back into the present. She picked up a piece of rose-coloured soap in the shape of a flower blossom, and savoured its delicately perfumed fragrance. It's incredible, she thought, comparing it in her mind to the family-sized economy bar they used at home. All those years, and Dad had never once—not once—hinted at the opulence he had left so irrevocably behind. She shook her head slowly back and forth, marvelling at him; at the hardness of his life; at its romance; at his quiet strength.

Later, calmed by the long, luscious bath and the tea Joséphine had promised—brought in a silver pot, with toasted, buttered bread—she decided to stretch out on the bed for a much-needed nap. Joséphine had reported that her grandfather was resting, and she had three hours before dinner at eight.

It seemed she had barely closed her eyes before Joséphine was back: 'But where are your evening gowns, *mademoiselle*?'

Camille forced her unwilling eyes open, and then burst into laughter. Joséphine was the picture of despondency, staring at the four sorry dresses in the wardrobe and gently biting her lower lip.

'In America no one wears long dresses except for

special occasions,' Camille said. 'I don't even have one.'

'It must be a strange country,' commented Joséphine.

'No, not really,' said Camille, jumping out of bed, 'just more casual.' The nap had refreshed her immensely. She even felt deliciously contrary. How had she ever let that overbearing Antoine cow her?

Despite Joséphine's protests, she deliberately chose her oldest dress, a white cotton shirtwaister, to wear for dinner. Casually, even carelessly, she swept her hair up in a knot. Who was there to impress? No matter how she dressed, she could never match Eugénie, and she was obviously of no interest to the aloof, supercilious Antoine. Not that she wanted any interest from him.

Just as she reached the bottom of the staircase, Antoine emerged from the drawing room. The elegance of his white dinner jacket accentuated his lean, tall frame. 'My sweet little cousin,' he said in that mocking tone of his, taking in her plain, unfashionable attire with sardonically flashing eyes. 'I see I should have mentioned we dress for dinner. Perhaps you would care to change? Henri can instruct the cook to delay preparation.'

Staring up at him, she was aware of a peculiar, frightening excitement running through her nerves as she took in his handsome features and his suave, sophisticated air. She lifted her chin and, with a great effort, achieved a cool formality as she answered him in her flawless French. 'It won't be necessary, my dear cousin. I don't have any formal clothes, but then'—she paused deliberately—'what would you expect from a girl who is the daughter of a peasant?'

To her satisfaction she could see him flush, even through his tan. So he was human after all. Taking advantage of his momentary confusion, she slipped past him to the entrance of the drawing room. The interior of the high-ceilinged room was splendidly furnished. There were settees of deep purple velvet trimmed with gold, and straight-backed, polished wooden chairs, hundreds of years old. Lovely porcelain ornaments of a sort she had never seen before graced marble-topped tables placed tastefully about, and thick Persian rugs lay on the rich, wooden parquet floor. An enormous crystal chandelier, which hung from the centre of the ceiling, was reflected in the massive, gold-framed mirror over the marble fireplace.

She took a deep breath, tried to look as if this were not the most beautiful room she had ever seen or ever hoped to see, and walked confidently in. As she expected, there was no sign of anyone who could be her grandfather. Eugénie, in a long, plum-coloured gown set off with a choker of pearls and diamonds, looked exquisite. That, too, was as expected. She was posing gracefully on a settee near the fireplace. A slim young man in a white dinner jacket, who looked remarkably like her, leaned against the mantel. He glanced up at once when Camille walked into the room.

'Ah, this must be the mysterious cousin from America?' he said in slightly accented English.

'It's not necessary to speak in English, Edouard.' Antoine's sardonic voice came from behind Camille. 'My cousin speaks perfect French . . . when she has a mind to.'

Eugénie languidly lifted her eyebrows. 'Your cousin must have many hidden talents of which we are unaware.' She spoke coolly. There was nothing in her tone to indicate embarrassment.

'Antoine, you must introduce me,' said Edouard, handing Camille a delicate aperitif glass he had filled for her from a cut-glass decanter.

'Thank you,' she murmured, taking the glass and pretending she didn't notice his eyes moving down her body. She took a small sip. It was a very good dry vermouth.

'Of course,' said Antoine, without expression, pouring himself a glass. 'Camille, this is Eugénie's twin brother, Edouard.' He took a seat next to Eugénie. 'Perhaps I ought to warn you, he's a notorious ladies' man.'

'Antoine!' Edouard feigned an injured expression. 'Your pretty little cousin might take you seriously.'

Antoine's face looked stern. 'I meant her to,' he said, looking directly at Edouard.

Edouard, unabashed, grinned at Antoine, then smiled openly at Camille. Glancing over the rim of her glass as she drank, Camille saw an unmistakable glint of anger in Antoine's eyes as he stared at Edouard. She was angry and confused. What business was it of this haughty man if another male found her attractive? Was it so unbelievable? Unsure of how to behave in the centre of tension between them, she breathed a quiet sigh of relief when Henri took that moment to enter the room and announce dinner. Relationships back home were nothing like this; they were simple and understandable, without intricate undercurrents and subtleties. The sooner she got back there, and away from these people, the better. The thought of home made her remember why she was here.

'Isn't my grandfather joining us for dinner?' she asked Antoine.

'He's not feeling up to it,' he answered, politely offering his arm to her in order to escort her into the dining room.

'His illness isn't serious, is it?' she asked, aware again of the strange excitement running through her at Antoine's nearness.

'My uncle is in his eighties and his heart is poor. He could live two more years, or he could die tomorrow.' Antoine spoke in a quiet voice, so as not to be heard by the others behind them. 'But surely,' he said in a tone as hard as steel, 'you knew that before coming.'

Camille's mind filled with sudden understanding. Somehow, he had got the idea from somewhere that she was here to establish a claim to her grandfather's estate. No wonder he was hostile. But he couldn't be more wrong! She had to get him alone at the first opportunity and convince him of just how wrong he was.

By the time the four of them were seated at the glittering table set with exquisite gold-rimmed china and delicate, handblown crystal, Camille's poise began to wear thin. She regretted her childish choice of dress. She wouldn't have looked half so ridiculous surrounded by these ultra-sophisticated people from another world, if she had chosen her best dress and had worn her hair down. Yet even as she was blaming her looks for her lack of ease she knew she wasn't being honest with herself.

It was Antoine who was destroying her equilibrium. She was acutely aware of him sitting across from her. Although she avoided looking directly at him, she could sense his brooding, hostile eyes fastened on her. It was as if the nap that refreshed her senses also allowed them to absorb the full force of his magnetism, a magnetism that somehow set her heart racing and her limbs trembling.

This is just great, thought Camille with grim humour. Here's the first man I find myself attracted to, and he looks at me as if I've just crawled out from under a rock.

After Henri had served the first course and left the room, Antoine—obviously finding his duties as host more onerous than usual—was the first to speak.

'This is your first trip to France, isn't it?' he asked.

'Yes,' Camille answered, controlling the tremor creeping over her body. Even his voice, clipped and grim, played on her senses.

'Do you think it will live up to your expectations?' he drawled, his mouth twisting mockingly.

'I never thought I would come here, so I have formed few expectations,' she said, her voice wavering slightly.

'But surely,' Edouard interjected, 'when your father talked about his country to you—'

'My father's country is the United States,' Camille retorted, 'and he never speaks of France.'

All three of them were startled by her vehemence. Camille instantly regretted her impulsive, defensive statement—even though it was true—as she caught Antoine and Eugénie exchanging amused glances. She had given them another opportunity to laugh at her expense. Feeling gauche, awkward, and sick at heart, Camille stared miserably at her plate. To her surprise and gratitude, Edouard smoothly and diplomatically changed the subject, asking Antoine a question about the approaching harvest.

Somehow, Camille managed to survive the ordeal. Although Antoine's glowering, disturbing presence played havoc with her emotions, and Eugénie pointedly ignored her altogether, Edouard adroitly kept up a steady, rather charming patter, directed for the most part at Camille. And, she thought ruefully, as course followed delicious course, she had never tasted and enjoyed so many new and exciting dishes before—not that her nervous stomach allowed her to do more than politely sample each one. The fine wines were more familiar, but only as rare treats. Never had she drunk them in such copious amounts.

Afterwards, when Antoine suggested adjourning to the drawing room for liqueurs, she excused herself, honestly pleading exhaustion, and fled to her room.

No matter what any of those people thought of her, she decided firmly, she wasn't going to leave Château Villon without seeing her grandfather. And she was solaced by the thought that as soon as Charles Deslandes saw how out of place she was in this environment he would probably hasten her departure for home, where the feelings Antoine de Breze aroused in her would naturally cool and fade. She congratulated herself on her level-headed good sense.

Ten minutes later she was undressed and drifting off to sleep with an unaccustomed lightheadedness from the many wines. Barely awake, and luxuriating in the silk sheets and down quilt, she was determined to thrust all thoughts of Antoine from her mind. Yet she could picture his features with such unnerving clarity that she knew it would take more than wishful thinking to banish him from her dreams.

CHAPTER TWO

JOSÉPHINE pulled back the heavy curtains, flooding the bedroom with light. Half awake, Camille opened her eyes and was momentarily puzzled by the rich lavender silk-covered quilt in incongruous contact with her old cotton nightgown. She sat up with a start as the events of yesterday came back to her, then flushed as remnants of appallingly sensual dreams of Antoine flashed through her mind.

'Pardon, *mademoiselle*. I let you sleep as long as I could.' Joséphine approached the bed with a loaded tray, fortunately seeming not to notice her heightened colour.

'What time is it?' asked Camille, pushing back her dishevelled hair and arranging the covers so that Joséphine could set the tray up over her lap.

'Almost noon, *mademoiselle*.'

'What!' An early riser by inclination as well as necessity, Camille could not remember a time when she had slept even until ten. Clearly, she was still operating on California time. And she had drunk far too much of the wonderful *vin de Bourgogne*.

'You have been sleeping like an infant despite all the noise,' said the maid, setting the tray over Camille's knees and pouring heavenly-smelling coffee from a silver server into a fluted cup so thin she could see the dark liquid through its sides. Joséphine poured only half a cupful, then filled the rest with steaming milk from a small ceramic pitcher, turning the coffee a light hazel brown. 'Your *café au lait, mademoiselle,*' she said.

Camille sipped the surprisingly delicious mixture and bit into a buttered croissant. She had had croissants before, but never one that quite literally melted in her mouth. 'I didn't hear a thing,' she said. 'Has it been noisy?'

'Oh, yes, *mademoiselle.*' Joséphine came closer and whispered conspiratorially, her good-natured face full of concern. 'I'm afraid Monsieur Antoine and Monsieur Deslandes had words this morning. Shouting, doors slamming . . . and with Monsieur Deslandes so weak.' She shook her head sorrowfully. 'I do not know what things are coming to.' Again she shook her head, this time more quickly, as if to clear her mind, '*Eh bien, mademoiselle*, you had better hurry. It is not a good thing to keep the master waiting.'

'What?' said Camille, with the cup halfway to her mouth. 'Is Monsieur Des—I mean my grandfather—waiting for me?'

'*Mais oui,*' said Joséphine. 'That is why I have awakened you.'

Thirty minutes later, only partially fortified by her breakfast, Camille stood with a sinking heart outside the set of white double doors with their intricate golden filigree. She took a deep breath to shore up her strength, and turned one of the porcelain handles.

Expecting to enter a sick room, she was surprised to find herself in a library. The walls, except for the fireplace and the window areas, were lined with ceiling-high bookcases. Ornately tooled leather bindings with gold lettering gleamed dimly on every side. The room was sparsely furnished, containing only a few wing-backed chairs of dark leather and an imposing desk in one corner. The overall effect, though austere, was tranquil and soothing.

Near the fireplace sat two of the wing-backed chairs. In one of them, warming himself by the fire, sat an aristocratic old man, his back as straight as the chair itself and his head high with an almost military bearing. Only the shawl spread over his legs and the pallor on his face indicated that Charles Jean Deslandes was not a well man. Except for his white hair and deeply lined faced, Camille might have been looking at her own father.

'Come in, child, and shut the door. You're letting in a draught.' His voice was much like her father's, but his French was far more beautiful—elegant and clearly enunciated.

'I'm sorry,' apologised Camille meekly, closing the door softly behind her. Tentatively, she sat down on the edge of the chair he indicated to her.

'I do not bite,' he said sternly. When she didn't reply, he went on: 'I suppose that idiotic father of yours has filled you with all sorts of horror stories about me?'

'No,' said Camille, her quick temper rising, 'he has never talked about you at all.'

Her grandfather's eyebrows shot up, and Camille thought she saw a glint of respect in his hard eyes. 'That is even worse,' he said. His gaze softened. 'Let me come quickly to the point. I was wrong to throw him out, and I wish to make amends.'

Camille was totally disconcerted. She had prepared for all sorts of scenarios—including having to beg—anything but this calm, matter-of-fact apology. She sat wordlessly and stared at her grandfather.

'I am not a well man, and I do not expect to live very long.' He spoke flatly, obviously not asking for sympathy, because he held up his hand as Camille started to speak.

'Antoine de Breze is my late wife's grandnephew and your second cousin. He was raised as my heir; he loves this estate as much as I do. He has worked hard to manage it, and he will inherit it.' The old man spoke challengingly, as if he dared Camille to argue. Then he put his hand to his brow and sank back against the chair, suddenly weary and old. 'And yet I cannot rest until I make some restitution to your father.' In a softer voice, he added, 'He, too, loved Château Villon.'

He shifted his gaze from Camille and stared into the fire. She could hear her heart pounding in the silence. When a burning log snapped she jumped, and hoped her grandfather hadn't noticed. After what seemed like for ever, when she was beginning to think he was dozing, he finally looked back at her.

'Antoine is a good man,' he said slowly, 'a good man. He's enamoured by that woman'—the way he said 'that woman' told volumes—'but he'll get over it. Once he gets tired of looking at her he'll discover she has a brain the size of a grape.'

Camille was both astonished and amused, but she couldn't follow the direction of her grandfather's thoughts. What did Antoine's love-life have to do with her or with the loan?

Her grandfather saw the confusion on her face. 'You are puzzled?' he said. 'Do not worry, you need not concern yourself with preparations. It is all arranged. We will have a private ceremony the day after tomorrow.' He leaned over and patted her arm with a dry, parchment-like hand. 'Antoine will make you a fine husband.'

Camille could only stare at him blankly. Had she heard him right? Was her grandfather senile, or crazy? Was this an insane joke? He couldn't possibly be sitting there discussing a marriage between her and a man she had met only yesterday—a man who, for all intents and purposes, seemed to hate her. She must have misunderstood.

He appeared to read her thoughts. 'I have not taken leave of my senses, my dear,' he said with a grim smile. 'I understand that in America young people have childish, romantic notions of love and marriage, but in France—in good families, at any rate—such foolishness is not allowed. That is why they are good families. I have kept Antoine from marrying for many years, waiting for you to reach a marriageable age and, let us say, a co-operative inclination.'

Despite the enormous implications of the statement, Camille finally got back the power of speech. 'You planned this!' she gasped. 'IMBEC, the Morans . . .'

'*Certainement*,' he laughed. 'Did you not think it unusual that a large corporation would buy a winery and then refuse to honour a contract to purchase the premium grapes it needed?' He chuckled again and added, 'IMBEC is a French corporation. The board of directors was delighted to help a major stockholder with a delicate family affair.'

'It's impossible,' she said stonily. 'I can't marry a man I don't love. My father would be horrified if he had any idea of your plan. He'd starve before he'd agree to this. . .' her voice faltered '. . . this scheme!'

Charles Jean Deslandes looked at his bewildered granddaughter mercilessly. 'That is why you are not going to tell him until it is done.'

'Not tell him!' Camille exploded. 'If you think for one minute—'

'Now, now,' he interrupted, 'you are not looking at this the right way. Through this marriage your father will indirectly gain back his inheritance. That is good, no? Antoine will get a wife of good blood— Deslandes blood. That too is good, *n'est-ce pas?*' Then he added menacingly, 'I can make quite sure that your father and Bernard lose their precious land— you do not want that, do you, *ma petite?*'

He paused to let the threat sink home. 'I do not want it either,' he continued. 'It would cause me great pain. Besides,' he added wryly, 'you will fall in love with Antoine, eventually—all women do.'

Camille desperately tried another tack, barely believing the conversation was real. 'He'll never agree to marry me. He doesn't even like me.'

'Nonsense, child,' her grandfather said airily, dismissing her objection. 'I must admit, however, that we had a small disagreement when I told him about it this morning . . .'

'You've already told him he has to marry me?' She was mortified. Antoine must have felt his suspicions about her fully justified. If he hadn't utterly despised her before, he certainly did now. For a reason she didn't understand, the thought not only embarrassed her, but hurt her deeply.

'Antoine is a practical man and will do as I say,' her grandfather said. His gaze travelled over her figure, objectively appraising her. Camille blushed. 'You'll attract him, I imagine,' he went on, 'that is, as soon as we get you some presentable clothes. I'll make the arrangements for your shopping this afternoon.' He closed his eyes for a moment. His face had taken on an ashen cast. 'I'm tired now, child. Run along. I will see you at dinner.'

Speechless, Camille fled to her room. Obviously, she wasn't going to be able to convince her grandfather to abandon this crazy plan—not without risking the sacrifice of her home. Surely though, Antoine must have some influence with him. He certainly had an incentive, she thought, with an irrational pang. Why would the handsome, eligible Antoine de Breze settle for a country bumpkin who didn't even know how to dress, when he could have instead the gorgeous Eugénie Jusserand—brains or no brains?'

'I couldn't possibly wear this!' exclaimed Camille as she viewed her reflection in the dressing room mirror. The form-fitting bodice of the evening gown plunged dramatically, showing a great deal more of her breasts than she had ever revealed before.

'*Mademoiselle* will look elegant and quite fashionable,' said the *propriétaire*, Madame Courbet, eyeing Camille critically. 'You have a beautiful figure, but like most young American women, you don't know what to do with it.'

Her tone said Camille was not to worry; Madame Courbet would see to everything. Had Camille's esteemed grandmother not frequented Madame Courbet's Christian Dior boutique in Dijon for many years before her untimely death? And had she not always been well pleased? Now, Monsieur Deslandes had instructed Madame Courbet to see to Camille's wardrobe—with no expense spared.

Camille looked back into the mirror. The dress certainly was a dream. Emerald green chiffon, lined with matching silk, clung to the curves of her body, then gently flared into graceful swirls to the floor. Her eyes, high-lighted by the rich colour, seemed greener than they ever had before. 'It's beautiful,' said Camille thoughtfully, 'but isn't it a little too . . . old for me?'

'With your hair in that pony tail and no make-up on, perhaps,' agreed Madame Courbet, 'but leave that to me. Marcel, my coiffeur, is superb. As a favour to me, he'll take care of that later this afternoon. Now, put on this black one. You have excellent shoulders and should not be afraid to show them.'

After Camille had tried on a succession of evening gowns, Madame Courbet chose the green one and three others, despite Camille's protests that she would never have the courage to wear them and that, even if she had, there would be no occasion; she would, after all, be returning to America very soon. Undeterred, Madame Courbet brushed aside her objections. 'This is enough for a start,' she said, 'but you will have to come in regularly in the future. Perhaps at the beginning of every season, when the new designs come in.'

For a start, thought Camille in amazement, looking at the pile of new garments—the gowns, two afternoon dresses, a beautifully tailored woollen suit, two cocktail dresses, and a sinfully sensual welter of silken underwear, peignoirs, and diaphanous négligés.

Things had rapidly got out of hand. Just an hour after her interview with her grandfather, the housekeeper had announced that Pierre had the car out and was ordered to take her shopping. She demanded to see her grandfather, but he was indisposed, and Antoine wasn't expected back until dinner. Camille didn't know what else to do but go. And to be honest, it sounded like fun to shop for a long dress; she had never even tried one on. But all of this! Her grandfather was sure to think she was going to go along with his ridiculous scheme.

Madame Courbet's voice drew her out of her reverie. 'I've instructed your chauffeur to drive you to Marcel's. Mademoiselle will look *ravissante*,' she said, leading her to the door.

The beauty salon looked nothing like the drab, businesslike one next to the supermarket back home. A young receptionist immediately escorted Camille to the back, past richly papered walls graced with heavy, gilt-framed mirrors. Stopping in front of the biggest mirrored station of all, Camille was placed under the care of an effusive, delicately featured young man. Full of apprehension she watched him brush her long hair.

'On you, long hair is very beautiful. Don't be afraid that I'll cut it all off,' he said, noting the concern on her face as he took up the scissors. 'But it is the tiniest bit *too* long.'

'But then won't I have to take a lot of time with it?'

Marcel pursed his lips and tipped his head. 'Only a little, with a curling iron, because when the weight is gone there will be some natural curl.' Deftly he went to work. After cutting and shampooing her hair, he brushed it and then blow-dried it into soft waves.

'It is beautiful, *n'est-ce pas?*' asked Marcel, stepping

back with a flourish and spinning her chair towards the mirror.

Camille raised her eyes to the mirror, and her breath caught in her throat. Her hair, thick and luxurious, cascaded to her shoulders, the ends curling softly. When she turned, it swung provocatively, catching the light and gleaming with the richness of gold. She was actually beautiful; beautiful and elegant. With the green gown, and with this hairstyle, she could rival even a woman like Eugénie for a man's attention. Which she had no intention of doing, she reminded herself.

'It certainly makes me look more mature,' she said, keeping her tone nonchalant. Marcel looked crestfallen, and Camille let some of her excitement show through. 'It's beautiful,' she said with sincerity, 'really beautiful.'

Marcel brightened. '*C'est parfait!*' He turned and motioned to an impeccably groomed older woman behind a counter nearby. 'Now Marie will show you how to apply make-up in the most effective manner.'

Marie brought over a tray holding a varied assortment of tiny containers. 'Do you use make-up, *mademoiselle*?' she asked severely, selecting a foundation colour that matched Camille's skin.

'Lipstick, sometimes, but usually I just don't have the time,' she answered.

'You must *take* the time. You could be very beautiful with just a little effort. Besides,' Marie lectured, 'it doesn't take long once you learn how. Close your eyes and lean back.'

Camille did as she was told, and was surprised when Marie said she could look just ten minutes later. A hint of rouge curved her cheeks to her temples, giving her cheekbones a high, classical appearance, and somehow making her throat more slender and graceful. Rather liberally applied mascara lengthened her lashes and made them incredibly full, and the touch of green on her eyelids set off her eyes to perfection. Most striking of all—and just the least bit shocking—were her lips, made invitingly soft and lush by moist-looking, plum-coloured lipstick. She couldn't help tingling with excitement.

'You see?' asked Marie.

Camille nodded. 'It looks wonderful.' And sexy, she added to herself, not without a glow of pleasure.

It was almost dinner time when she returned to the château. The butler, Henri, helped Pierre unload and take the astonishing assortment of boxes to her room. Joséphine, who had been waiting there for her, squealed with pleasure when she saw them, and squealed again at Camille's new look. As Henri was leaving, he took a flat velvet box from his coat. 'Your grandfather would like you to wear this tonight, *mademoiselle*,' he said without expression, then withdrew and closed the door behind him.

Oblivious to Joséphine's enraptured chatter as the maid unwrapped packages, Camille slowly opened the box. Nestled in a bed of grey silk lay an antique emerald and diamond necklace. Camille knew nothing about gems, but she knew that no costume jewellery had ever burned with so deep and luminous a lustre. She stared at them in shock.

'*Mademoiselle*,' exclaimed Joséphine, clearly awestruck, 'the Deslandes emeralds! I have not seen them in ten years!' She looked perplexed. 'On Madame Deslandes's death, she left instructions that they be given to Monsieur Antoine's future wife.'

Camille closed the box. 'There's been a misunderstanding, Joséphine,' she said calmly to the maid. 'My grandfather is under the impression I'm going to marry Antoine.'

Joséphine clapped her hands in delight. 'Oh, Monsieur Antoine, he's so handsome! How wonderful—'

'I'm not going to marry Antoine,' broke in Camille with exasperation, 'I barely know him and I'm certainly not going to marry a man I don't love.' Even if she was physically attracted to him, she amended ruefully to herself.

Her enthusiasm not the slightest bit dampened, Joséphine continued with Gallic fatalism. 'All women fall in love with Antoine, and you will be better for him than that Eugénie Jusserand.'

'What's wrong with Eugénie?' asked Camille, her curiosity piqued.

'She is obviously after his money . . .' Joséphine said, then clamped her mouth closed.

'And . . . ?' said Camille.

The words came out in a flood. 'And her manners towards the servants are terrible, atrocious, unladylike!' She wrinkled her nose expressively.

'I can certainly see that she might be arrogant,' Camille said, 'but I don't understand about the money. She must have plenty of her own.'

'It is not my place to say, *mademoiselle*, but according to her chauffeur things are not going well with her father's business. Many times,' she said, beginning again to unwrap the clothes, 'things are known in the servants' quarters before anywhere else. Besides, even if it is not true, such a woman never has enough money.' Joséphine lifted the lid of the box that held the green evening dress. '*Merveilleux!*' she exclaimed. 'You must wear it tonight. It will be perfect with the emeralds.'

That was hardly surprising, thought Camille wryly, since her grandfather must have told Madame Courbet to choose a dress that would match them. How carefully, how irritatingly, he had planned it all. She momentarily considered refusing to play her role in his little charade, but after the excitement of the day she longed to look glamorous and elegant for just one evening. Also, at the back of her mind was the desire that Antoine—and, yes, his snob of a girl-friend as well—should see her in her new sophistication. Then let them try to ridicule her looks again in some future tête-à-tête.

'Yes,' she said firmly to Joséphine, 'it will be just fine with the emeralds.'

To her surprise her grandfather called for her personally. It was the first time she had seen him standing, and he was even taller and straighter than she had thought. At first he stood gazing at her so silently that she began to wonder if he were somehow offended. Gently he touched first the necklace and then a lock of her hair. 'I didn't notice this morning, *ma chérie*, how much you look like your mother. She was very beautiful. If I had been younger I would have fallen in love with her myself.'

He took her arm to escort her down the stairway. She noticed that, erect as his posture was, he used his other hand to carefully support himself on the banister. 'You are more beautiful than your mother, however,' he continued, 'because you have the grace and carriage of a Deslandes.'

'Grandfather . . .' She halted at the foot of the

stairs, hearing the sounds of many voices from the drawing room. She turned nervously towards him. 'There are guests? Joséphine didn't say anything—'

'A small surprise.' He shrugged. 'Just a few close friends. They would be hurt not to hear first-hand of the engagement.'

Camille gasped. 'Grandfather! You're not going to announce it *tonight*?'

'And why not?' he said, pretending surprise. 'It is settled, is it not?' He smiled, patting her hand. 'Antoine is in for a big surprise when he sees that the little duckling has turned into a swan,' he chuckled.

She didn't have time to reply before they entered the brightly lit room. The 'few friends' turned out to be a crowd of fifty. There were people everywhere, mostly with glasses in their hands.

Antoine emerged to meet them. Camille felt an exquisite, unaccountable thrill of triumph when she saw his defiant, angry look turn to one of amazement. He quickly got control of himself, however, and by the time he met them his expression was nearly as indifferent as usual.

'Well, Antoine, what do you think?' her grandfather asked. 'Your little second cousin from America is quite beautiful, no?'

'Quite,' said Antoine with a perfunctory smile, but Camille could see that he was impressed in spite of himself.

His great-uncle could see it, too, and laughed. 'You'll have plenty of time to monopolise her later. Now I want to get her a glass of champagne and give our friends a chance to meet her.'

As soon as she had murmured a conventional greeting to Antoine, Monsieur Deslandes proudly began to introduce her to the others. They seemed so much alike she found it impossible to remember any names. Everyone was dressed with flawless taste, and everyone had the clear complexion, the casual posture, and the supremely polite, condescending manner of the very rich. The men and older women complimented Camille effusively, and the younger women were icily polite. Camille wondered if many really were in love with Antoine, as everyone seemed to take as a matter of course. Considering the effect he had on her in just one day, she reflected wryly, it wasn't so unbelievable. With his looks, his sexual magnetism, and his position as heir to one of the world's great wineries, she thought, he probably has women falling all over him in droves if he so much as looks at them. Not this one, though, she vowed firmly to herself.

Eugénie was absent, which was a mild disappointment, but Edouard was there, and he greeted her with frank admiration. Her grandfather left her with him briefly while he joined several elderly men arguing vigorously about the merits of a new technique for increasing crop size from the conventional four thousand plants per acre to four thousand five hundred.

Edouard whistled appreciatively when Monsieur Deslandes was gone. 'It's a good thing my sister decided her headache made it impossible for her to come down.'

'Why?' asked Camille, sipping her champagne.

'She's convinced herself Antoine will never marry a girl who looks like a farm girl.' Edouard threw back his head and laughed, then lowered his voice and said, 'For the first time I really envy Antoine.'

'You don't seem terribly concerned about your sister,' she remarked, puzzled.

Edouard shrugged. 'My sister is spoiled. She takes herself too seriously.' He tossed off the rest of the champagne in his glass, and a waiter refilled it at his nod. 'I suppose one could say I'm spoiled too, but no one has ever accused me of taking life too seriously. There are too many pretty women to admire—and occasionally a truly beautiful one, such as the one I'm looking at now.'

Camille couldn't help smiling. 'Antoine was right. You *are* a ladies' man.'

'And to Antoine, that's some sort of crime—the fact that I'd rather be talking to a fragrant, seductive, maddeningly beautiful woman, than be on my knees in the dirt, grubbing around the vines.' He moved closer. Camille, flattered but a little wary, stepped back.

'That's why Antoine dislikes me, you know,' he said. 'He thinks women, like the other pleasures of life, should be relegated strictly to the hours after five o'clock. Worse, he thinks everyone should be like him.'

'And what is he like?' asked Camille, oddly defensive of Antoine, in spite of his maddening view of women as playthings—if Edouard was right about him, and she rather thought he was.

'Antoine de Breze? Obscenely industrious. He lives for this estate alone. It's everything to him.' Edouard shook his head mournfully. 'And with his looks, what a waste. The women, fools that they are, adore him and ignore me.'

Camille laughed. 'Oh, yes, I'll bet they do. You're a rogue, Edouard, but I like you. Of course,' she added quickly, 'I'd never trust you alone.' She glanced around the crowded room, looking for Antoine, and found him at once, staring at her with brooding eyes from the far corner.

His eyes narrowed when he saw her looking at him. She couldn't help but note his assertive, masculine jaw, and his mouth clamped into a hard, fierce line. She could see both ruthlessness and mockery in his face, and she quailed inwardly as she sensed the danger that emanated from him. Suddenly she realised that the charade had gone on long enough.

'Will you excuse me, Edouard?' she said. She moved rapidly through the clusters of people. Perhaps she could quickly have a few words alone with Antoine. He had to stop her grandfather before he announced the engagement. Noticing her come his way, Antoine detached himself from the group he was with and met her halfway, steering her out of the French doors and on to the deserted, moonlit terrace.

'I certainly underestimated you, my little cousin,' he said curtly. 'It didn't take you long, did it?'

'You're all wrong—'

He didn't let her finish. 'A beautifully conceived plan, but not wholly successful in the execution, was it? I imagine your father will be shocked to find out that instead of his little daughter completely duping a sick old man, she's only been able to get back half his inheritance—and she's had to buy it back with her own body, at that.'

For a moment she held her breath like a child in shock; then she raised her hand to slap him.

He caught it easily, and the other one as well, pulling her roughly against him. 'Not here, *ma petite*, someone might be looking out of the windows.'

She felt his fingers crushing her wrists, and was frighteningly aware of his hard, powerful body through the thin silk of her dress. She trembled, her green eyes glittering as brightly as the jewels at her throat. Her gleaming young breasts rose and fell against his chest as her heart beat tumultuously.

'You're as mad as my grandfather,' she cried, her voice shaking with fury and fear. 'If you don't let me go I'll scream!'

'What? And shock those within who think we've escaped for a lover's embrace?'

He loosened his hold, however. Camille could see that he too was breathing hard. 'For Château Villon I would marry Medusa herself,' he said, very softly, yet the quiet tones of his voice held so much menace Camille instinctively shrank back. His hands tightened on her wrists once more. 'However, I must confess that after seeing you tonight, obeying my uncle won't be quite the hardship I thought.'

She opened her mouth to speak, but it was covered savagely by his. For a few frightening seconds she thought he would cut off her breath for ever. He pulled his mouth away briefly, then kissed her again, deeply, irresistibly. She writhed, trying to free her hands. Never had she been kissed like this before. She shuddered in embarrassment as she felt her body respond shockingly. Appalled, she wrenched her head away. 'Damn you! Let me go! I hate you!' she whispered passionately. 'Nobody wants your stupid estate, and God knows I don't want *you*!'

Antoine was disconcerted by the obvious ring of truth in her voice. Abruptly he let her go and then stepped back. She was relieved to see the old sardonic look in his eyes replace the lust that had been there a moment ago. Camille massaged her wrists, glad she didn't bruise easily. 'All I came here to ask for was a loan, one that we had every intention of paying back in a year. Everything else—including this crazy marriage—is Grandfather's plan.'

'What do you mean?' Still hostile, Antoine also sounded intrigued.

'Grandfather even engineered our money problems,' Camille said.

Antoine laughed mirthlessly. 'You expect me to believe that?'

'I really don't care what you believe,' she replied stonily, 'but it's true.' She told him about the interview she had had with Monsieur Deslandes that morning.

When she finished speaking, she waited breathlessly for assurances from him that he could change her grandfather's mind. Instead, he stared down at her with unfathomable eyes. As the silence lengthened he sensed her fear and suddenly smiled with barbed amusement.

'Frightened, aren't you?' he said curtly. 'And so you ought to be. If you're not lying, my uncle has gone to considerable trouble to arrange this. We're in a trap.'

'Surely you can do something,' she gasped.

'Actually, I find your professed fear of an imminent marriage to me quite touching,' he drawled sarcastically, 'especially since you couldn't wait to dress the part of the future Madame de Breze.'

'You're totally mistaken if you think I'd want to be your wife for a second,' she retorted heatedly, then added, echoing his sarcasm, 'I just wanted to repay you for making your country cousin feel so *welcome* yesterday.'

Antoine looked down at her, only half believing her, but she could see her barb hit home.

'We can't afford to go into this now,' he said, frowning. 'For tonight we have no choice but to follow my uncle's lead.' He glanced back at the château. 'Right now it looks as if dinner is about to be served.'

Long buffet tables had been placed at the end of a large ballroom opening on the far side of the entrance hall. The magnificent chamber was lit by three massive chandeliers fitted with hundreds of candles for the occasion. Mirrored walls reflected and multiplied the wavering flames endlessly, so that the room was alive with thousands of flickering, glimmering pinpoints of orange light. Even the parquet floor gleamed and glimmered and seemed to undulate. Camille had never seen anything remotely like it. The entire company, filled champagne glasses in hand, had lined up to toast them. Camille's grandfather beamed when she and Antoine entered together. Henri, waiting at the entrance, ceremoniously handed them two fluted, long-stemmed champagne glasses.

Monsieur Deslandes lifted his glass dramatically, and all the eyes in the room seemed to follow the gesture. '*Mes amis*, I have the very great pleasure of announcing the engagement of my granddaughter, Camille Marie Deslandes, to my grandnephew, Antoine Jules de Breze.' Camille was amazed to see his eyes glisten. 'May they have a happy marriage and a long life together. *Felicitations!*' he cried, and drank deeply.

'*Felicitations!*' echoed fifty voices, and fifty brimming glasses rose.

Camille glanced nervously at Antoine beside her. She was startled to find him smiling into her eyes. He raised his glass to her. 'To my future bride,' he said quietly, touching his glass to hers with the soft chime of crystal on crystal. Bewilderment shone in Camille's eyes as she drank the champagne. It was hard to believe that this was the same man who had growled at her so ferociously on the terrace just a few minutes ago. He was giving a terrifically good performance as the enamoured, attentive suitor. Before she had time to speculate further, her grandfather appeared at their side.

'Your young lady has had, I think, an unusually exciting day.'

Camille smiled to herself. That was the understatement of the year.

'I think it is time I provided her with some sustenance—that is, if you can possibly allow me to take her from you for a few moments.'

Antoine bowed his head deferentially, and was immediately snapped up in conversation by a horsy-looking woman on his left.

Monsieur Deslandes solicitously heaped Camille's plate with an assortment of delicious-looking foods from the overflowing tables. The pleasing sounds of happy people enjoying good food and champagne drifted around them. Somewhere a small orchestra was playing a Viennese waltz. It was all extremely pleasant.

As soon as Camille saw the food and smelled it, she realised she was famished; she had had nothing since her breakfast croissants.

Her grandfather seemed delighted with her youthful appetite. He probably thinks I've capitulated, too, she thought crossly. Only the knowledge that their conversation could be overheard restrained Camille from setting him straight.

'Do you have good French food at home, *ma petite?*' he asked, picking at the scanty portion he had placed on his own plate.

'Not really. My mother died before I was old enough to learn to cook, and Dad tries, but to be honest he's all thumbs in the kitchen.'

Monsieur Deslandes laughed with amusement at the thought of his son cooking at all, much less well.

'I can see now why he never felt comfortable in a kitchen,' she said, looking around and laughing too. Underneath, she marvelled once again at what her father—her dear, ageing father in his sweatstained workmen's shirts—had so uncomplainingly given up.

'Bernie has taught me how to cook some good French stews—a wonderful *pot-au-feu*—but nothing like this.' Cautiously, she tried a little piece of a long, tender dumpling covered with a pale sauce. It was the most delicious thing she had ever tasted. 'It's wonderful!' she exclaimed. 'What is it?

The old man smiled. 'You have excellent taste. It is a *quenelle*. The sauce on it is made from lobster.' He ate a tiny piece of his own.

'It's exquisite,' said Camille, taking another bite. 'And this little pastry with sauce inside?' she asked, drinking champagne from a glass that seemed to refill itself.

'That is a *bouchée à la reine*—the mouth of the queen. It is filled with creamed sweetbreads.' He looked at her for a long time without speaking. Camille, slightly embarrassed, sipped her champagne.

He spoke with sudden vehemence, almost angrily. 'You look so beautiful tonight, child. How much I have lost!' Then he smiled with infinite sadness. His old, dry hand touched the back of hers. 'But, *ma chérie*, for the little time I have left, I have gained something back. Who knows, perhaps my son will return, too.'

For the first time she felt a flood of sympathy for the old man, but her resolution didn't waver. She would have to get out of this arranged marriage, this impossible, eighteenth-century farce he had concocted. But not tonight. Tonight was his night; let him enjoy it.

Besides, Camille had to admit she was unexpectedly enjoying herself, too. She felt light as a cloud and exquisitely happy. She didn't know if it was the champagne or the feeling that she—not Antoine—had somehow won that battle on the terrace. She didn't care. She was beautiful tonight and she was going to savour the moment.

Antoine suddenly appeared behind her, asked her grandfather's permission, and swept her into his arms and on to the dance floor. Several other men sought out partners and followed his lead, so that soon the whole candlelit room was spinning and lilting to a Strauss waltz.

As they danced, Camille was electrifyingly conscious of Antoine's hand on her back and of the hardness of his chest against her breasts. The memory of the kiss on the terrace flashed through her mind and her cheeks flooded with colour. As if he read her thoughts, a flame of roguish amusement kindled in his eyes.

'When a woman flowers into a beauty, she has to expect to arouse lust in men,' he taunted.

'She should also be able to expect them to keep their hands to themselves,' she replied coolly.

He grinned sardonically and pulled her even closer. For the first time Camille thanked her father for making her take those hateful dance lessons when she was sixteen. She felt as though she were a lovely winged creature, soaring and gliding effortlessly. Antoine was staring down at her when she stole a glance up at him. He was preposterously good-looking. How romantic it would all be if they were really in love and engaged. It wouldn't be a farce then, she thought; it would be a fairy-tale.

'You seem to be enjoying yourself,' he said, his voice full of mockery.

'I am, actually,' she said on impulse. 'This environment is so foreign to me I feel like Cinderella at the ball. Tomorrow, though,' she added firmly, 'I have every intention of turning back into a middle-class, American girl on a short visit to some rather *peculiar* relatives.'

'I heartily wish you could,' he said with vehement and unmistakable sincerity. 'We need to talk. May we go outside?' He gave her a satirical smile. 'I promise to keep my hands off you.'

'If we must,' she assented reluctantly, ignoring the small jab of pain caused by his obvious eagerness to be rid of her.

The moon had risen higher, and the terrace was bathed in a cold, white light, so that the marble statues and tall, neatly trimmed bushes were ghost-like and ethereal, less substantial than their shadows of inky black. The music floated from the ballroom, thin and faraway. Antoine led her to a stone bench with carved cherubs on the sides.

'The engagement's been announced. There's nothing we can do but go through with it.' He spoke in a clipped, grim voice. Standing before her, bathed in the cold moonlight, he might have been a marble statue himself. 'And, frankly, it will be in your best interest as well as mine to go along. Charles Deslandes doesn't make idle threats, and he can be ruthless when crossed,' he informed her bluntly.

Wordless, she stared up at him.

'He has little time to live, and it will make him happy. When he dies we can divorce and take up our lives where we left them.' Antoine paused. 'Frankly, I'm not interested in my great-uncle's liquid assests—which are extensive, by the way. I have a private fortune of my own. So those assets will provide a generous settlement for you . . .'

Camille started to speak but he cut her off before she could get out a word.

'. . . but the estate and winery are another matter. When your father scorned them, your grandfather turned to me to carry on the family tradition. Unlike your father, I accepted the restraints such a responsibility entailed and worked hard for him and for myself.' His voice hardened and the suppressed power of it sent a shiver down Camille's spine. 'Understand me well. I will let nothing and no one stand between me and what is rightfully mine.'

Camille was more frightened than she would care to admit by his icy, menacing tone, but she responded tartly.

'You can keep the estate and the money,' she said, bridling at his imperious assumption that he could buy her co-operation. She could see he didn't believe her, but she couldn't care less.

She was acutely distressed at the thought of being trapped into intimacy with this man. Her intuition warned her that she was on dangerous ground. After that kiss, a man of his experience would know she was physically attracted to him. Probably, he even looked forward to amusing himself at her expense, she thought with a mixture of fear and chagrin.

'I'll go through with it,' she said slowly, 'but only for my father's and Bernie's sake.' She fought down a sense of rising panic. 'And only on one condition. It will be a marriage in name only.'

Her words brought a glitter of sardonic amusement to Antoine's eyes. 'A marriage in name only. What a quaint phrase.' Insolently, his eyes roamed her slender, curvaceous body. 'Surely I can expect some privileges, as a husband.'

'Nothing!' she snapped. He looked so smugly confident of his sexuality that she wanted to hit him.

He shrugged his broad shoulders. 'How childish. There might have been some delightful ways to pass the time. But if you insist.' The faint music stopped. 'Shall we return to our guests?'

CHAPTER THREE

THEY were married in a quiet, private, late-afternoon ceremony two days later. Eugénie did not attend. With Edouard, she had left the morning after the engagement was announced. She had been aloof, but not unfriendly to Camille. She had, in fact, been icily magnanimous. Camille surmised that Antoine had wasted no time telling her of their businesslike arrangement. She didn't know why it disturbed her so to think Antoine might really be in love with Eugénie and not merely infatuated. The one thing she did know for sure, reflected Camille wryly, was that any woman would be a fool not to wait for a man like Antoine—provided, of course, that she loved him. And Eugénie Jusserand was no fool.

As soon as the ceremony was over and the two of them had received the surprisingly hearty congratulations of the estate workers and household servants, Camille retreated to her suite. She was startled to find every horizontal surface covered with fragrant bouquets of long-stemmed roses. To her dismay a small table laid with a brilliantly white tablecloth and set for two had been placed in the sitting room. She was further discomfited to discover that her plain silk sheets and pillowcases had been replaced with hand-embroidered ones edged in antique lace. Joséphine had laid out her most elegant peignoir and nightgown and beside it lay a disconcertingly masculine velour robe of deep blue.

54

Disquieted, Camille stood transfixed in the middle of the bedroom.

'Oh!' she exclaimed, jumping in alarm, as two strong hands grasped her around the waist from behind. She spun around to find Antoine staring down at her. He gave her a wicked smile at the sight of her transparent embarrassment.

'Antoine! You startled me!' She blushed furiously at being caught staring at the bed, and was alarmingly conscious of Antoine's hands, again resting on her waist. Tall and distinguished in the perfectly tailored grey suit that did little to conceal the physical strength of his trim, muscular body and broad shoulders, he let his eyes roam her slender figure, outlined under the thin silk of her lacy, cream-coloured afternoon frock. Camille felt her cheeks turn still warmer.

'You look so delectably alarmed, *ma petite*,' he said, as he continued to smile at her naïvety. 'Are you sure you don't want to renegotiate our contract? I think I might enjoy furthering your—shall we say—education,' he said, his voice full of mockery.

He stood there, towering over her, virile and strong—a man who might stir any woman's senses.

Flustered, her heart racing uncontrollably, she stepped back out of his grasp. 'No thanks. I'll pick my own instructors,' she snapped, turning and walking to the sitting room. 'I'm glad you find the situation so amusing, but I don't.'

He laughed in delight at her retreat. Joining her, he casually sat down on the settee and put his feet up on the tufted footstool. 'You're such a lovely innocent,' he teased, loosening his tie.

Camille looked nervously around the room. His

banter made her furious. But the intimacy of their situation was already sending warning signals along her nerves and she was desperately anxious to keep their relationship on a smooth, even, impersonal level. Innocent she might be, but she understood enough about men to know that it would be a good idea to get off this subject. As soon as she found out about logistics that is, she thought, absentmindly biting her lower lip in consternation. She asked haltingly, 'We aren't expected to . . . to share this suite, are we?' She avoided looking in his direction.

Antoine answered in that maddeningly amused, sardonic tone. 'At least tonight we are.'

Camille looked up in time to see him toss down his tie and unbutton his collar. 'I didn't mean tonight—I expected we'd have to pretend to . . .' her voice trailed off. The small, sensual glimpse of his hairy chest revealed in the open throat of his shirt unnerved her.

'You mean for the duration of our arrangement?' he said.

'Yes.'

Antoine shook his head and pointed to a small, unobtrusive locked door in the far wall which Camille had assumed was a storage closet. 'That connects to my suite.' He pulled a delicate brass key out of his pocket and indifferently tossed it to her.

She caught it and couldn't help sighing in relief. 'Then no one will really know how long you stayed here tonight. You could even leave now,' she added hopefully. She felt entirely defenceless alone with him in the suite, especially because she wasn't absolutely sure of her ability to keep him at arm's length.

Antoine feigned an injured expression. 'Alas, how

true. Denying me your bed is one thing, *ma chérie*, but surely you're not going to be so cruel as to banish me without dinner.' He was laughing under his breath and she seethed, staring at him.

'After dinner, then,' she said tersely.

There was a discreet knock on the door. A beaming Henri entered, wheeling a serving car piled enormously high with delectable-looking dishes and an oversized, silver champagne bucket into which were tucked two magnum-sized bottles of champagne.

Camille could barely restrain commenting until Henri left.

'That's enough food and drink for a week!'

Antoine's eyes travelled again up and down her body, 'If we were in love, *ma petite*, or if I hadn't promised not to take advantage of your . . .' he paused and added in a mocking tone '. . . shall we say, vulnerable position, it might have been a week before I let you escape from this room.'

He laughed as her colour rose again, and she came close to throwing a vase full of roses at him. Only the thought of the mess being discovered by the servants restrained her.

'You're being a brute, Antoine de Breze!'

His handsome, mobile face assumed a contrite expression, that didn't fool her in the least. 'You're right. I'm sorry.' He smiled. 'Truce?'

His smile was so charming, so polished, that she knew intuitively that he had had considerable experience with women. Even if it was all relegated to after five o'clock.

'All right,' she muttered unwillingly after a moment. She wondered if it would ever be possible to

win a verbal sparring match with him. She doubted
it.

'Now, shall we partake of some of this extraordi-
nary meal?' he asked, getting up and deftly opening a
champagne bottle.

'And after we eat, you leave?'

'*Certainement*,' he taunted. 'I wouldn't dream of
doing anything else.'

Their unexpected marriage created a huge sensation. Although she should have suspected it would,
because of Antoine's wealth and power in the French
wine industry, the wave of curiosity that ran through
the newspapers stunned her.

Camille called her father immediately to inform
him of the situation, fearing an American paper
might pick up the story. Jean Adrien's anger exploded through the transatlantic cable lines. For the
first fifteen minutes of the call Camille feared both for
the cable and her ear-drums. Finally though, she
calmed him down and explained her and Antoine's
real relationship. Happily, he not only accepted the
situation, he found it amusingly appropriate.

'It serves my old devil of a father right,' Jean
Adrien said, chuckling.

Camille was relieved. She had been more worried
than she realised about how her father would react.

'It does, really,' she agreed, 'but you know, Dad, I
can't help but like *Grand-père*. He's been so sweet to
me and everything—once he got his way, that is,' she
added with a touch of asperity in her voice. 'I guess
he's got it in his head this marriage will make things
up to you . . . and to me.'

'To tell you the truth, to me it doesn't matter any

more, honey—too much water has passed under the bridge. But I wouldn't be honest if I didn't confess to you that I feel as if I've robbed you. So I do thank him for what he's trying to do for you, even if I heartily disapprove of his method.'

'Don't be silly; you haven't robbed me of anything,' Camille retorted tartly. 'I had a perfectly happy childhood—except for the loss of Mom, of course. And you and Bernie mean more to me than any old estate.'

Jean Adrien laughed, his voice more cheerful. 'Thanks, honey. Even so, maybe it's not a bad thing for you to spend some time in France leading the life of leisure. You've already put in enough work around here to deserve a break. Bernie and I can take care of things until you come home.'

'Don't either of you work too hard,' she couldn't help cautioning, trying to sound content. She didn't want to depress her father by telling him that she wouldn't want a life of leisure, and that she already missed working in the vineyard.

Camille was hit with a wave of homesickness as she put down the telephone and took in the wealth and luxury of the furnishings around her. Already she was finding out that riches could be confining and oppressive.

In public, Antoine was playing the attentive husband to perfection; in private he acted more like an arrogant, maddening big brother, a big brother who was prone to lecture her on what was expected in her new role as Madame de Breze. This, as far as Camille could tell, consisted of nothing more than walking about dressed to the hilt, looking dignified, visiting other estate owners' wives, and eating too much. Antoine himself spent most of the day on estate matters, something Camille longed to be involved in, too.

At least, she thought, thankful for small favours, her grandfather's health and the coming harvest precluded a honeymoon and put off her introduction to Parisian high society. She felt far too young and unsophisticated, despite her outward, naturally elegant bearing, to cope with that.

There had been, though, a succession of local afternoon receptions for the bride, and intimate dinner parties for the two of them. To Camille's relief everyone—except an occasional mother of an unmarried daughter—had been quite nice. Jean Adrien had been well-liked and well-remembered in the neighbourhood, and she could see that people thought it right and proper that she had been brought from America to marry Antoine.

Despite his provocative banter on their wedding night, he had scrupulously kept his distance. For the first few days she was relieved. Then she found herself awakening in the cool of the night, disturbingly conscious of his presence on the other side of the door—disturbingly conscious that she might be falling in love with him.

With all of the social engagements, it was two weeks before Camille had an opportunity to break away for a solitary walk through the great Villon vineyards. As she strolled slowly down the rows between the vines, she could feel a hint of autumn coolness in the breeze wafting through the Côte-d'Or.

Harvest time was close at hand, a hectic, exhilarating time, when no one slept except in snatches. At home in America, vintners and their families worked side by side with the hired pickers. It was a magical time, if the weather were right, filled with the light-hearted gaiety of a holiday. Picking the grapes was fun; everyone was inspired by the thought that this might be the harvest that would produce not just a good wine, but perhaps a great wine.

She forgot for a moment that she wasn't in her father's vineyard in California, and absent-mindly took off her sandals so she could feel the cool, rich dirt under her feet. Of course, if the weather were bad . . . no, she thought like a good vintner's daughter, she wasn't even going to entertain the idea in case it brought bad luck. She couldn't help but cast an anxious glance towards the horizon, though, to look for rain clouds. She was searching the perfectly clear sky so intently for the faintest hint of a cloud that she didn't hear Antoine come up behind her.

'Camille!' he said tersely, gesturing at her feet, 'what if one of the workers saw you?' He stood towering over her. She could see the muscles in his arms ripple under the close-fitting blue denim work-shirt as he rested his hands on his hips. His shirt, opened because of the heat, revealed a thin gold chain and medallion hanging around his neck and nestling in the dark hair of his tanned chest. As she had on their wedding night, she found it a disquietingly sensual sight.

'If you can't remember your own position,' he said curtly, 'you can at least think about mine.'

'*Oui, mon capitaine,*' she said sarcastically, her anger rising at his tone, then feeling instantly contrite. After all, she wasn't in America and conventions were important to the French.

Besides, something far more important was at stake. She brushed off her feet and slipped her sandals back on. 'Antoine,' she said softening her tone, 'we need to talk.'

'I haven't a moment to spare now,' he said abruptly. 'I'm up to my ears in work and I have a million things to do before we start harvesting.'

'But that's what I wanted to talk to you about. I'd like very much to help.'

'Help!' His mouth twisted in derision and irritation. 'What, may I ask, could you do?'

'I can do lots of things.' Her voice shook slightly. 'At home Bernie gave me responsibility for my own section of the vineyard—'

Antoine threw back his head and laughed. 'Bernard Fouquet, possibly the best vintner and winemaker in the world, bar none, let you make decisions on your own?' he cried mockingly. 'Make-work is what it was; make-work to get you out of his hair. He probably countermanded every order you gave.' The laughter fled from his eyes. His voice turned flinty. 'But I'm not running a few Californian acres and selling the grapes for others to make the wine. I have a large estate to oversee, and winemaking besides. I don't have time for play. Besides,' he added irritably, 'you are Charles Jean Deslandes's only granddaughter, and, moreover, you are now Madame de Breze. No. Absolutely not. It would be completely unsuitable.'

There was a long moment of tense, dangerous silence between them. Camille's anger came close to exploding at his summary dismissal of her suggestion.

'Look, Camille,' Antoine said more evenly, using

his most infuriatingly condescending big-brother tone, 'Why don't you have Pierre take you shopping for a new dress for the dinner François is giving us tonight? Wouldn't that be fun?'

'New dress!' she snapped angrily, no longer able to contain herself. 'I have two I've yet to wear. I want something constructive to do! I can't believe all you Frenchmen want from your women is for them to sit around and look decorative! A vase would do just as well!'

'Don't get temperamental on me at this particular moment,' he warned, 'and I don't want to hear any more about this.' The direct command shocked and startled her.

'You can't give me orders like that! Who do you think you are anyway, my hus . . .' she broke off in confusion.

'Husband?' he said icily. 'Yes, for most intents and purposes.' His tone was cold, but the anger in his voice turned to amusement. 'And if I had more time, I'd turn you over my knee and give you the spanking your father should have given you years ago.'

'Beast!' Camille muttered at his retreating back. 'Oh!' She jerked a leaf off the nearest vine and shredded it in frustration.

Antoine's dismissal of the notion that Bernie had given her any responsibility didn't surprise her. Her father had reacted the same way when Bernie first proposed the idea. It had been hard for Jean Adrien to adjust to the fact that his daughter had developed a better 'vintner's sense'—that special intuition needed to be a first-class vintner—than he had. Something that could never be taught, it was a sort of sixth sense that could only be nurtured as Bernie had delicately nurtured Camille's. And now, 'vintner's sense' or not, for the first time since she was a child she was to stand idly by while everyone around her had a role in the most exciting event of the year.

Until Camille was five, her mother—a soft, delicate woman, always beautifully groomed—had kept Camille close under her wing and dressed her as a miniature replica of herself. Then Marie had died, and neither her father nor Bernie had the faintest idea of what to do with her. Camille wanted nothing more than to tag along behind them while they tended the vines; it was much more fun than playing in the house. Her first harvest job had been no more than placing the grapes in the basket for Bernie after he cut them, but she loved it. The frilly dresses were soon gone entirely, replaced by jeans and T-shirts, and Camille revelled in her new freedom. The men stopped worrying about her and, indeed, as she grew older, they became increasingly dependent on her help.

Now, thought Camille in disgust, watching a stocky figure come towards her down the row, she had somehow been put back into the china-doll routine. As the man approached Camille, he politely pulled off his dusty, black beret.

'*Bonjour, madame.*' He was a short man in his mid-fifties, and there was something about him that reminded Camille vaguely of someone, but she couldn't think whom.

'*Bonjour, monsieur,*' she responded shortly. Although she was angry at only one Frenchman in particular, she didn't feel terribly friendly towards any of them.

The man examined one of the rich purple clusters

near them and plucked off a couple of grapes, rolling one between thumb and forefinger, and handing the other to Camille.

'Ready soon,' he said in a friendly, uninterested way.

Camille abstractedly weighed the grape in her hand, squeezed it, tasted it. 'Another two hot days like this, at the most,' she responded mechanically, her mind elsewhere.

He grunted non-committally, but there was a hint of surprise on his weatherbeaten face. 'Good year.'

'It would have been better if someone had been a little more heavy-handed with the pruning shears,' she commented, then was suddenly ashamed at the haughtiness of her tone. The man was twisting his beret in his hands, apparently confounded by her coldness.

'I don't believe we've met,' Camille said, smiling and putting some warmth in her voice.

'Rémi Fouquet. I am the estate manager, Madame de Breze.' He was in truth confounded, but by her words, not her manner. She had judged the grape exactly as he would have, expertly and accurately, and it grated against his Burgundian pride, not to mention his masculinity, to have this juvenile from America express his own thoughts. His uncle's last letter had told him to expect it, but still—

'Fouquet!' she responded in delight. 'You must be Bernie's—I mean Bernard's nephew!'

Rémi nodded his head. 'I wish he had come with you. It would have been good to see him.' He shrugged expressively.

'He writes from time to time, but that's not the same thing. *Mon oncle* is in good health, no?'

'Oh, yes, he can run circles around me, even at seventy.' Camille was surprised to hear that Bernie corresponded with his family in France. It was something he never mentioned. Perhaps, she thought, he didn't want to remind her father of unpleasant memories.

'Bernard Fouquet was the best vintner and wine-maker in all of Burgundy. He was an artist. But we were not surprised when he decided to go with Jean Adrien to America.' He smiled softly. 'When Jean Adrien was little, he was like a shadow—following Bernard everywhere. He was like a son to him.'

'He is a son to him now.' Camille said. 'Until I came here I didn't know that he—or my father—had been connected with Château Villon. I don't know how they could have kept such a secret. I didn't even know my father's real name. I suppose you know,' she added shyly, 'my father took your family name when they emigrated.

'It was a great honour for our family,' Rémi said with sincerity. 'Of course, Monsieur Deslandes went purple with rage.' He chuckled. 'He would have let me go, and all my brothers too, if he could have replaced us. But I was Bernard's assistant manager, and next to him, the best winemaker in the district.' He smiled wryly. 'My uncle taught me everything he could—and I am a very good vintner,' he said defiantly. Then, mournfully: 'Yet, I do not have his flair; I admit it. Our wines are now *Premier Cru* not *Grand Cru.*'

Camille was at a loss for words, and feeling vaguely guilty.

Rémi brightened. 'My uncle writes to me that he

sees much promise in you. It's good, this marriage, for Antoine and the estate.'

Camille blushed. 'Bernard must have exaggerated when he wrote—'

'My uncle never exaggerates,' he said bluntly. 'Besides, I confess I was testing you.' His eyes twinkled, and it was like looking at Bernie. 'Two days at the most and these grapes will be ready, and I complained just yesterday to Pierre, who pruned this section, that the vines were carrying too much fruit.'

'You mean . . .' Camille stopped and laughed. 'That was tricky.' She sighed and said, 'I wish you could convince Monsieur de Breze that I know something about growing grapes. I'd like to help.'

Rémi chuckled. 'One needs diplomacy in dealing with the French. We are not used to having our wives advise us in our work. Give me time and I'll see what I can do. Meanwhile, I am here because Antoine sent me to see if you would like me to show you the cellars.'

Camille was astounded. 'I'd love to if you can spare the time,' she said, marvelling that Antoine had arranged something so nice for her after her temper tantrum.

'Time! For you I would make time,' he said gallantly. 'We are practically family, no?'

'Absolutely,' agreed Camille, laughing.

'Come. I have some men racking a little of last year's gamay, and we can check on their progress.'

Camille was very pleased at the 'we'.

She was so enthralled by the twelfth-century wine cellars and her new friend that she forgot about the evening's dinner invitation, and was late returning to the château to dress. Dashing up to her room, she saw with relief that Joséphine had drawn a bath for her and had laid out all but a dress.

'*Madame!* If you don't hurry you will be late,' the maid scolded.

'I know,' said Camille throwing off her shirt and blouse on the way to the bathroom. 'Pull out my black gown, will you, please? I want to look as nice as possible tonight.'

She had decided Rémi was right. She would have to learn diplomacy. If the French were a nation of diplomats, she would get her way a lot more easily by being subtle. She hoped so, anyway, and if not, she wasn't above using a few feminine wiles, either. She smiled faintly as she hurriedly bathed.

Madame Courbet had been right. The black gown showed off her shoulders and back to perfection. Behind, the dress plunged almost to her waist. Two thin straps held up the bodice, cut high just under her breasts, and criss-crossed across her back. The skirt flared smoothly to the floor, except in the front, where it was gathered, Empire-style.

Camille selected a large diamond necklace and matching earrings. Despite her protests, her grandfather had showered her with family jewels. When she privately mentioned to Antoine that she felt like an impostor accepting them even temporarily, he stilled her qualms with a common-sense answer. It would look strange if she didn't, and she might as well enjoy wearing them. At first it was fun, but unexpected images of Antoine some day admiring the same jewels on another woman began to intrude whenever she put them on. It was these streaks of jealousy that told Camille she had fallen in love with

Antoine Jules de Breze . . . fallen hard in just two short weeks.

Tonight, as she examined her dress in the mirror, she owned up to the fact that although Antoine might be physically attracted to her and would probably enjoy seducing her if she gave him half a chance, he showed no sign of falling in love with her.

Therefore, for her pride and self-esteem, she was determined to hide her own feelings. And to do that, she needed some absorbing task to throw herself into, some responsibility for the harvest. It would help to take her mind off him. And she was not above scheming to get her way.

'Ah, *madame*, you look *ravissante*,' cried Joséphine, startling Camille out of her thoughts.

'*Merci*, Joséphine. I hope Antoine will think so.'

Misinterpreting Camille's statement, Joséphine responded reassuringly, 'Don't worry, *madame*, if Monsieur Antoine is foolish enough to still pine for that dry stick of a Eugénie Jusserand, he won't for long.'

Camille began to check Joséphine's enthusiasm and loyalty to her—some day, after all, Eugénie might be her mistress—but she decided it would be useless. Besides, it was awful to think of poor Joséphine staying on if that event occurred. She would just have to make sure Joséphine was placed in another good position before she returned to America.

Her grandfather was reading by the fire in his study when she stopped by to wish him goodnight. His expression softened as he set down his book and looked her over with complete approval.

'Enjoy yourself tonight, *ma chérie*.'

'I wish you were going with us,' said Camille, kissing him on the cheek. At least she didn't have to hide her growing affection for *him*.

'Henri is bringing me a small dinner soon. I know you young ones find it hard to believe, but at my age,' he said, patting the leather-bound volume, 'a good book and a quiet evening are great pleasures.'

She smiled. "Goodnight, then, *Grand-père*. I suppose you need your rest anyway," she said playfully, glancing at their half-finished chess game. They had fallen into a habit of playing briefly after lunch, ever since Charles Deslandes had discovered his granddaughter was a worthy opponent. 'I don't know how you're going to save your queen,' she added teasingly, making a quick retreat before he could reply.

Antoine was waiting for her in the drawing room. His dark eyes moved slowly over her, mockery in his gaze, along with something else, something indefinable. 'A vase would never do as well,' he said slowly.

'I apologise, Antoine,' she said contritely. 'You were busy this afternoon and I picked a bad time for a talk.'

He lifted her chin with his fingertips, and she fought the confident sexual magnetism he so arrogantly displayed. It would only be natural—if she gave him half a chance—for a man of his wealth and background to see her as a new plaything. And *that* she had no intention of becoming.

'You looked very beautiful this afternoon when you were angry,' he said in his off-handed way. 'Did you enjoy your tour of the cellars?'

Camille smiled and said evenly, 'Very much.' She stepped back from him, afraid he would hear the wild beating of her heart at his touch. She recoiled at the thought that her body might betray her if he ever turned the full force of his charm on her. But, distasteful as the thought was, there was more than a little truth in it. Forewarned is forearmed, she thought grimly. Keeping her voice cool and impersonal, she said, 'It was generous of you to suggest it to Rémi, when I know there were more important things for him to be doing.'

He took the white fur stole she was carrying, and she turned so he could drape it around her shoulders.

'Tonight, as long as you keep your shoes on,' Antoine said with ironic amusement, 'I don't have to worry about the de Breze image. The little gypsy of this afternoon looks like a most elegant young woman.'

He ran his hand gently down the curve of her neck. 'You know, Camille, there are times—'

'We're going to be late if we don't hurry,' she said nervously, alarmed by the way her knees went suddenly weak at his touch. 'As guests of honour, that wouldn't do.'

The small dinner party was a pleasant repetition of the others. François Chevillot was a charming and witty host, and his dark, vivacious wife Hélène greeted Antoine's new bride warmly.

'I hope you enjoy the food tonight, Camille,' said Hélène confidentially as they sat down to dinner. 'François has high blood pressure and must watch his diet, so our chef has learned to cook in the style of the *nouvelle cuisine*.'

'I'm sure I shall,' Camille assured her hostess. 'I've heard a lot about it and I'm dying to try it. Besides, I've never eaten such rich foods. I'm afraid

I'm going to start looking like a *soufflé*. The puffy kind.'

'It's hard to keep one's figure,' commiserated Hélène, 'especially when the little ones start to appear.' Hélène, the proud mother of three, flashed a meaningful glance at Antoine, then back to Camille.

Camille felt her cheeks flood with colour. Hélène, not insensitive, smiled and changed the subject, thinking how sweet Antoine's new bride was.

The *nouvelle cuisine* was a delight: poached trout stuffed with a scallop *mousseline*, with a garniture of leek and mushroom. Afterwards, as usual, the ladies retreated to a salon to drink their coffee and to chat about fashions, while the gentlemen lingered in the dining room to talk wine. For once, Camille left the more interesting discussion without regret. Let Antoine have his masculine wine talk. It always relaxed him and made him expansive. When they got home, he might be in a good mood to listen to reason about giving her some responsibilities.

'What a day!' he said, closing the door behind them when they arrived home two hours later.

'Would you like me to pour you a glass of brandy?' Camille asked, smiling.

'No, thanks. Got to be up at dawn tomorrow. Sleep in as long as you want. Goodnight.' There was a glint in his dark eyes. Amusement? But he was striding up the stairs before she had had time to utter a single, carefully rehearsed word.

Biting back an angry retort, Camille stamped upstairs to her own room and threw her stole down in disgust. She stood furiously in the middle of the room, her hands on her hips. That infuriating man! He *knew* she wanted to talk to him! And he was

probably laughing at her right now. She changed
angrily into a nightgown and peignoir, but the catch
on her necklace was stubborn. For a few moments
she struggled irritatedly with it, but soon gave up in
exasperation. If she had to, she would sleep with it
on. It was too late to call Joséphine, and she wasn't
going to give Antoine the satisfaction of asking him
for *anything*. On the other hand, she thought, it would
be one more opportunity to talk with him. He could
hardly refuse, and men did seem to be in their best
humour when they were fooling with silly mechan-
ical things. It was worth a try.

'Come in,' Antoine answered in a surprise tone
when she knocked at their connecting door.

He was in his shirtsleeves, taking off his cuff-links
at the bureau. The only light in the room was a small
lamp on the bureau top, and it threw his face into
craggy shadows above the brilliant white shirt. How
incredibly handsome he was! Camille was suddenly
frightened, and was not put at ease when Antoine
raised an eyebrow and silently raked her body with
his eyes, first moving slowly up it, lingering, and then
moving slowly down again.

She blushed, her cheeks burning. My God, she
was barely clothed! In her eagerness to manoeuvre
him into a talk, she had forgotten that she had
changed out of her dress. What must he think?

'I . . . I couldn't release the catch on my necklace,'
she stammered, miserably aware of how absurd she
sounded, 'and I didn't want to . . . to wake Joséphine
. . .' Her voice trailed off.

He slowly finished taking off his cuff-links, dropped them carelessly on the table and moved across
the room to her. She started to turn so that he could

reach the clasp, but he caught hold of her shoulders, his fingers biting into her flesh. '*Mon dieu!* Don't be so bloody stupid,' he said fiercely. 'Look at you!'

Her peignoir had fallen open when she half turned, revealing her slender body in its thin, semi-transparent gown. Antoine looked down at her hungrily.

'Are you really so naïve?' he demanded fiercely. 'Do you really think you can stroll into a man's room like that and not expect . . . ?'

She stared at him wide-eyed, struck dumb at the passion she had so inadvertently evoked in him.

Antoine's eyes blazed, and his face came down towards her, his mouth covering hers hungrily, forcing her lips to part under his long, hard kiss. Her heart was hammering against her chest as his hands moved possessively down her back and then under the flimsy bodice to cup the soft roundness of her breasts.

In shock, she tried to think how she could get out of this, but he pulled her roughly on to the bed. His hands were clasped bruisingly on her shoulders; his lips, firm and sensual, explored her mouth, her cheeks, her soft throat, the tender cleft between her breasts.

'Antoine, please,' she murmured. 'Let me go, or I'll—'

'What,' he said harshly, 'call the servants to complain that your husband is forcing himself on you?' He kissed her passionately, lingeringly.

Dazed and terribly aroused, she was aware that his powerful, heavy body now pressed on hers; she felt his heart thundering against her chest; felt the hungry urgency of him; felt above all his lips moving over her, no longer brutal and hard, but soft, tender, caressing. A slow wave of ecstasy, insistent and irresistible, flowed over her. She shuddered at the stirring inside her, barely aware that she was now clinging to him, no longer resisting, her body instinctively arched towards him, folding like a house of cards.

Abruptly, Antoine pulled his lips away from her and laughed. 'That should teach you a lesson, *ma chérie.*' Gone was the passion; the old mockery was back.

Camille opened her eyes—she hadn't realised they were closed—and looked up at him, so dizzy she could hardly see. He was sitting up at her side, an easy, confident smile on his face. It was as if someone had doused her from head to foot with icy water.

'Why, you beast, this was all an act!' In fury she bounded to her feet.

Quick as lightning, he was after her, his hands clamped on her wrists.

'Now calm down,' he said, laughing as she struggled to hit him.

Realising it was futile, she stopped and glared at him indignantly.

'Speaking of acting,' he said, 'I noticed you've been all sweetness and light since our argument this afternoon.' He looked at her levelly. 'Now confess, you haven't given up on your little plan about working, have you?' He shook her wrists, but without malice, and demanded tauntingly, 'Confess!'

'I hate you! I hate you! Oh, how I hate you!' Camille whispered passionately.

'Let us hope that will pass once you've nursed your wounded pride,' he said scornfully. 'Otherwise we are going to have a difficult year or two. Get this through that pretty little skull of yours once and for all: no wife of mine—no matter how temporary—works.'

'Let me go!'

'Just one more thing, *chérie*.' His voice had gone husky and she could see the passion flicker in his eyes again as he stared down at her.

'I meant to frighten you. Let it be a warning never to try this tactic again to get something you want.'

'Antoine,' she said, 'I assure you that I did not—'

'There is a great difference between shamming a sexual passion one does not really have,' he said, his hands tightening again on her wrists, 'and giving in to a feeling one *does* have. I simply didn't resist my feelings. I cannot guarantee how it will end the next time you come to my room dressed like this.'

He looked down at her naked shoulders again, and Camille shrank back, but he only smiled and gently replaced a dangling silken strap on her shoulder.

'I'm going to go take a cold shower,' he said. 'I think I need one.'

He pulled her towards him, but this time he kissed her lightly and let her go. '*Bonne nuit, ma petite.* You have a lot to learn about men. Especially French ones.'

CHAPTER FOUR

FOR the next several days, Camille took care to avoid Antoine's company as much as possible, an easy task inasmuch as work claimed most of his waking hours. Despite her most determined efforts, her mind kept drifting back to the humiliating scene in his room. What mortified her the most was not that he had seen through her so quickly, but that he had deliberately waited until he had aroused her before ending that cruel hoax of a love scene. She would never forgive him! Her cheeks burnt with pink every time she thought of it. But, she thought defiantly, Antoine Jules de Breze had something to learn too—about American women. He might have won a battle or two, but he was going to find out the war had just begun.

Soon, even from the sidelines, Camille was caught up in the excitement. For more than a week the estate workers had been harvesting the pinot and gamay grapes on the valley floor, for the making of the red wines. The source of the great white burgundies, the chardonnay grapes planted on the terraces above the château, were only now becoming ready.

The grape pickers, old people and children alike, spread out across the vineyards, harvesting from dawn nearly to dusk. The men worked in shirts and pantaloons of blue, with rubber boots to their knees, and berets pulled low over their foreheads. The women were less uniformly dressed, but most wore

bright aprons and scarves, soon made more colourful
still by the brilliant purple juice.

One morning she took a walk along the upper part
of the hillside so that she could look over the
vineyards. Pausing for a moment, she watched seven
or eight groups of workers, moving slowly down the
rows with their baskets and clippers, picking grapes.
Lilting snatches of folk songs and bursts of laughter
drifted up. As in the Napa Valley, the hard work
seemed to make everyone happier and more ener-
getic—if it looked like a good harvest. And if, Camille thought miserably, one had something to do.

She arrived back at the château, but felt too
restless to go inside. Cutting across the terrace, she
aimlessly picked one of the paths that meandered
through the formal gardens. She came across the
stone bench with the carved cherubs on the sides,
where she had sat, listening to Antoine, the night of
their engagement party. How little she had realised
then, that living at Château Villon was going to be so
dull. Camille sat down on the bench and stared
ruefully at the full skirt of her afternoon frock, which
lay in graceful folds around her. What she wouldn't
give to be wearing jeans and tennis shoes and to have
back her old freedom.

'Still trying to avoid me?'

Antoine's voice startled her. He seemed to have
appeared out of nowhere. Bridling at the mockery in
his tone, she was silent for a moment, gazing up at
him, seeing his sensual, firm mouth, his casual,
relaxed stance, his hands resting lightly on his hips.
The memory of the feel of those hands on her skin,
the burning touch of his lips, made her back stiffen
and her cheeks flame.

His mouth took on a wry slant. 'Maybe I went too far that night, Camille, but you needed to be taught a lesson. After all,' he said, suddenly smiling broadly, 'I don't know why you find it so embarrassing to have responded to my lovemaking.'

'Must you rub it in?' she said stiffly, standing up and turning to leave.

He reached out and caught her arm, his fingers firm, and turned her towards him. 'Actually, it was a poor idea on my part,' he said glumly, 'because I haven't been able to get how beautiful you looked . . . and felt . . . out of my mind.' His other hand reached out and traced the line of her cheek.

'Stop it, Antoine!' she said shakily. 'I don't want you to touch me!'

'Don't be childish, Camille. I can tell you do, just by looking at you.' Passion flicked in his dark eyes. 'What's wrong with two people responding to a physical attraction? You wanted me that night and I've been kicking myself for stopping ever since.'

'Well, you've missed your one and only chance,' she retorted defiantly, and tried unsuccessfully to pull away from him.

'Have I?' he asked, tightening his grasp. His voice was low and husky as he pulled her up hard against him and kissed her slowly, searchingly, forcing her to open her lips to him, despite herself.

Camille was conscious of him with every fibre of her being, conscious of the muscular hardness of his tall lean frame pressing against her. 'Don't,' she begged weakly, when he moved his mouth from hers to kiss her ear and throat, 'you're not being fair.'

He pulled back and laughed softly. 'Perhaps I'm not.' He kissed her again, lightly this time, and let her go with obvious reluctance. 'But is it fair that I'm saddled with a bewitching female who's begun to haunt my dreams?'

Haunt his dreams! The words sent a surge of pleasure and hope running through Camille's veins. Could it be possible that Antoine was growing more interested in her? And could that interest develop from sexual attraction to love?

Antoine looked at his watch. 'It's getting late.' Abruptly he assumed a businesslike manner. 'I need to check on the crushing.'

Camille's spirits plummeted. He had dismissed her from his mind in a second. It was not a very flattering thought. She had just been put on a shelf like a porcelain doll.

When Antoine's mind turned towards business, he underwent a transformation. She had already seen him in action with some of their distributors and equipment suppliers. The ironic humour and casual air he adopted in social situations were not in evidence at such times. His voice would become cool, impersonal, and authoritative, and his face would assume an astute watchfulness. Château Villon wines might have experienced a small drop in quality under Rémi, but it had only resulted in a slight loss of prestige. The wines were still excellent and Antoine's business acumen kept the winery among the first ranks of what was a highly competitive market. It had not surprised her to learn that Antoine Jules de Breze was as highly respected as her grandfather. No wonder that the ageing Charles Deslandes had completely turned over the reins.

Camille, who knew a great deal about the growing of grapes in a small vineyard, longed to know more about the inner workings of a great estate like Château Villon. And yet here she was right on the scene, but denied access. It was too frustrating for words.

'I'll see you at lunch.' He paused for a moment when he noticed the sudden look of dejection on her face, then added, 'Or would you like to go along?'

Camille's heart leaped. 'Yes, I would.' She tried to sound nonchalant, but her voice was eager in spite of herself.

It was refreshingly cool in the *cuverie*, the large stone building that housed the vats. There the grapes were unloaded from the carts into the treading-vat, which burst the skins and discarded the stalks. Then the juice and pulped fruit were put into the huge, ancient wooden vats to start fermentation.

Her eyes sparkled with excitement as she took in the scene.

'One could tell you're a Deslandes just by looking at you,' commented Antoine dryly, watching her take it all in. 'Feel free to come and watch as often as you want . . . but don't get in the way.'

Camille choked down a retort. Even watching was an improvement over hanging around the château. 'Thanks,' she murmured demurely, managing to keep all traces of sarcasm out of her voice.

Antoine nodded, his mind elsewhere, and left her under the watchful eye of Rémi, who was directing the operation.

Over the next week, Camille took to dropping by the *cuverie* in the afternoons. Frequently she would find Antoine there.

'Winemaking is so much more romantic here than in America, and I'm not sure it's any less efficient,' said Camille to him one afternoon, raising her voice to be heard over the sound of the treading-vat. It was halfway through the harvest and things seemed to be going well.

'Oh?' Antoine said, not really listening to her. He was looking depressed and abstracted. Camille hoped it wasn't for the reason she thought it was.

She gestured to the horse-drawn cart that had just pulled up, and to the towering wooden vats. 'We use trucks and a lot of wineries have stainless steel tanks—nowhere near as romantic.

He momentarily brightened. 'I'm glad you appreciate tradition. It's very important to us,' he said, then added gloomily, 'I don't like this humidity.'

Camille had noticed it too, but had been hoping it didn't mean here what it meant in September in the Napa Valley. 'Isn't it usual this time of year?' she asked, clinging to a faint strand of hope.

He shook his head. 'No. And I smell rain no matter what the weather forecast said this morning.'

'Oh no,' exclaimed Camille, aghast. An untimely rain would, at best, lower the quality of the yield, for the thirsty plants would soak up the unaccustomed moisture and dilute the sugar in the grapes. And at worst, rain could cause the dreaded mould and mildew that turn the grapes rotten and unusable. Despite all the modern weapons against grape diseases and pests, a vintner still had no defence against unseasonable weather.

'*Oui*,' he muttered grimly, 'and we have just started to harvest the chardonnay grapes. We'll have to move quickly.' He deliberated with himself for a few moments, and seemed to come to a decision.

'Camille,' he said abruptly, 'would you please go ask your grandfather to release the house servants to pick grapes. We are going to need all the help we can get.'

'Of course.' She jumped down quickly from the barrel she had been sitting on.

Her grandfather issued the command immediately, having expected it. Fretfully he chafed at the limits his own health imposed on him. Camille calmed him down as well as she could, but she was restless and depressed herself.

The rooms, usually so bright and alive, were eerily silent without the servants. Even Henri, the butler, had declined a special dispensation from Monsieur Deslandes and headed to the fields with grim determination, notwithstanding his sixty-nine years.

The long, dull afternoon, spent distracting her grandfather with conversation and chess, and preparing a lonely supper for the two of them, finally faded into night. As Rémi had predicted, clouds had begun to gather. The workers lit lanterns so that they could continue on in the fields despite the dark. About ten, Camille heard the first raindrops strike the windows in her room. Fortunately, her grandfather had already gone to bed so, assuming he was asleep, he was at least spared from worry until the morning.

Opening the balcony doors, she stepped out. As far as the eye could see through the drizzle, hundreds of flickering lanterns swayed in the dark, on the hillsides and in the valley as well. People on the neighbouring estates were working through the night, too.

Camille could have screamed in frustration. The

easiest course was just to go to bed, but she knew
sleep was out of the question. With sudden resolve
she made up her mind. She wasn't going to go
rustling through the silent house like some ethereal
French countess petrified with the thought of spoil-
ing her manicure. She was going out to work with the
others. As for Antoine, she'd worry about him later.
He was too busy to check up on her anyway. He
hadn't even had the time—or the inclination—to
come home for dinner, though she had saved some
for him. No doubt he'd be out all night, so how was
he to know she wasn't in the house like a good,
obedient French wife?

She pulled out the bottom drawer of the wardrobe,
where her 'grubbies' had lain since her arrival. Her
plum-coloured St Laurent suit was flung helter-
skelter on the bed, and a few minutes later she
emerged from her room in jeans, cotton shirt, and a
scarf and nylon jacket to keep off the worst of the
rain. She found some gloves in the kitchen, and
strode determinedly to the front door, her heavy
work shoes clunking inelegantly on the polished,
parquet floors.

Rémi sighed. 'Monsieur Antoine is not going to like
it.'

'Just say I ordered you,' Camille said. 'Rémi, I
wouldn't even suggest it if I weren't an experienced
picker,' she pleaded, sensing a weakening of his
resolve. 'But I used to help lots of times at home. And
you know as well as I do, even having just one more
experienced hand working means saving hundreds
of pounds of grapes.'

'Monsieur Antoine is not going to like it,' Rémi

repeated, but this time with gloomy resignation. 'I could use another person in the upper terrace.' He motioned to one of the workers who was helping to unload grapes from a cart. 'Take Madame de Breze up to Claude and tell him to give her a section to pick—a whole section; she's experienced.'

With eyes as wide as saucers, the workman watched Camille pick up a basket and clippers. 'Thanks, Rémi!' she shouted.

'Thank me tomorrow, if I'm still alive,' he responded gruffly, but he was grinning.

Camille followed her guide up the narrow, rutted path. The rich soil, already turning to mud, clung to her shoes in sodden clumps, making walking arduous. Breathing fast by the time they reached Claude's area, Camille promised herself to get more exercise in the future. Just one month of life in high society and she was already out of shape.

The workman turned Camille over to a shocked Claude, doffed his hat shyly in her direction, and plodded back down the soggy track.

Camille could see that the area supervisor was sceptical about her usefulness, but pragmatic. Any help was welcome, even from the mistress of the estate. If she didn't turn out to be much help—as long as she didn't get in the way—she couldn't hurt anything.

He started her on an unpicked row, and in the flickering light of a nearby lantern, Camille went to work with a will, delighting in the feel of the plump clusters and envisioning another saved bottle of wine in each filled basket. A shy, sturdy fourteen-year-old named Jules was assigned to carry her filled baskets and those of the other pickers in the area to the edge of the terrace, where he unloaded them on to a cart.

She lost track of the hours and numbers of times Jules appeared to drop an empty basket and take away a full one. The drizzle turned to a soft, steady rain, drenching her to the skin. Her back began to ache from the endless stooping, but she was happier and more at peace than she had been in a long time. It was a joy to be doing something active and useful, and she had the substantial satisfaction of keeping up with the other pickers. She could see Claude's respect for her growing through the night as he assigned her to new rows.

'May I take the basket, Madame de Breze?' Jules asked shyly, adoration in his eyes. He persisted in asking her permission every time, though she had told him it wasn't necessary.

'Of course,' she answered, smiling, stopping for a moment to stretch and rest. She could see others had also stopped for a break.

Jules stood a moment looking down at his feet, then slowly pulled from his pocket something wrapped in a kerchief. Diffidently, he offered it to Camille.

'*Ma mère*'—he gestured towards a group of workers in the distance—'made it for you.'

Camille unwrapped the kerchief and was delighted to find a salami-and-cheese sandwich on thick slabs of crusty French bread. '*Merci*, Jules, this is just what I need. Thank her for me, will you?'

'*Oui, madame*,' he said, dropping his head shyly and leaving with the filled basket.

She ate the sandwich slowly, savouring every luscious bite.

'Claude, how does it go?'

Her heart nearly stopped in panic. It was Antoine, on his horseback tour of the work areas.

The two men were several rows away; Antoine was leaning down over the wet, lustrous neck of his mount to talk to the area supervisor. His slicker, gleaming in the rain, covered him like a flowing cape, but his head was bare, so this his drenched hair streamed over his forehead in heavy black locks.

Ducking down, Camille began working again, her fingers trembling. She strained to hear whether Claude was going to mention her—why hadn't she told him not to?—until she heard Antoine's horse clop wetly away. Thank God; Claude probably hadn't dreamt she was here without Antoine's knowledge.

Vastly relieved, and fortified by the sandwich, she continued working until a thin, watery gleam of light appeared over the hills to the east, when Claude sent her and half the other workers back home to rest. Proud that she had stuck it out, but very glad of the break, she started down the track without protest. Besides, if she made it back and changed, Antoine would never find out she had been out. Claude and Rémi would keep it to themselves if she asked them. Wet, tired, and stiff, with her teeth chattering from the damp dawn chill, she walked tiredly down the track, her eyes to the ground, looking for slippery patches.

She didn't see him until she almost stumbled upon the horse, and then she knew who the rider was before she looked up. Her stomach seemed to twist and sink when she raised her eyes to find Antoine looking down at her, fury contorting his handsome features.

Antoine de Breze swore in French, so softly she could hardly hear him, yet she quailed at the menace in his tone. Then she stiffened and stood defiant. After all, what could he do to her? Send her home to America? She had no objection. If he wanted an argument here in the rain, she was ready.

But he didn't want an argument. With speed and strength that overwhelmed her, he dismounted and lifted her to the saddle, mounting swiftly behind her. Digging his heels into the horse's sides, he guided it without speaking back towards the château. Camille struggled in a forlorn attempt to get down.

'Behave yourself, you little hellion,' he said through clenched teeth, tightening his arms around her.

She stopped struggling; his embrace was like steel. Against her, she felt the pressure of his hard warm chest, and tried to draw away from him, but he merely crushed her closer.

Dismounting, he grasped her around the waist and took her from the saddle, depositing her none too gently on the ground. Then, while holding her wrist with one hand, he secured the horse's reins to a railing with the other. Still he did not speak. As he pulled her up the stairs towards the threshold, she stumbled. Antoine gave a low, disgusted exclamation, gathering her up in his arms as if she were weightless, and carried her up to her suite. He set her down unceremoniously in front of the gold-flecked, wall-length mirror at the side of her marble bath.

'Look at you!' he said grimly. 'Filthy, bedraggled, wet to the skin . . . and your teeth are chattering.'

He roughly pulled off her sodden scarf, swearing tersely as he threw it on the floor. 'Take a hot bath.

I'm going to make us some coffee. It's time for us to have that talk and get this settled once and for all.'

Her green eyes wide—his tight-lipped, tense anger had her really frightened—she watched him leave and slam the door behind him. He was right about one thing. She *was* cold! She turned on the taps full blast, then stripped off her clothes with numbed fingers, and stepped gratefully into the hot water. Impulsively, she sprinkled in some of the fragrant bath salts that sat in a stoppered bottle on the rim. Feeling some of the stiffness flow out of her body as she stretched out in the soothing water, she lingered as long as she dared. She had no desire for Antoine to find her still there when he returned. Quickly, she blow-dried her hair until it fell in soft waves around her shoulders, and then securely tied her robe's belt around her waist.

Antoine returned, bearing a silver coffee pot and two cups on a tray, just as she emerged into her sitting room. He set the tray down on the table near the small settee and motioned to her to join him. Camille tentatively sat down beside him and watched him pour the coffee. She was relieved to see that the fury had drained out of him. He had showered and was wearing his velour robe, his dark hair damp and curling slightly at the neck.

'Are all American women as headstrong and obstinate as you, or are you an exception?' he asked, with no hint of humour.

'I couldn't just sit by and do nothing while everyone else worked!' She flung the words at him, then added softly, 'Besides, I didn't think you'd hear about it.'

Antoine flushed angrily. 'Hear about it!' he said

curtly. 'It's probably the talk of the whole valley right now.'

'Really, Antoine,' Camille retorted, 'I think most people will put it down as eccentric behaviour if they think anything at all. You can blame it on my barbaric American upbringing.'

Antoine glared back at her. 'Rémi Fouquet said almost the same thing when I asked him how he could let you do such a thing. What did you two do, rehearse your excuses?'

'We did no such thing. It was all my fault. Please, Antoine, don't take it out on Rémi. I practically ordered him,' she said pleadingly.

Antoine glared back at her, his jaw muscles tight and dangerous. Suddenly he laughed and his gaze softened, in that remarkable way he had of switching his anger off like an electric light. 'Why should I blame Rémi when I can't handle you myself? It's true; Americans do have a reputation for the unconventional, a reputation I am beginning to find out is well-deserved. Drink your coffee.'

Camille took a willing sip, unwinding as the hot liquid coursed down her throat. It had been laced with brandy.

'*Mon dieu*,' he murmured, brushing her hair away from her cheek as she bent her head over the cup again, 'you are a lovely handful.'

Camille put up a hand to push his away, but feeling a strange electrical tingle as her fingers touched his, she froze. 'Especially,' she said, forcing the words out, 'since you must have your mind on other things. Like the harvest. And *Eugénie Jusserand* perhaps?'

'Yes,' he mocked, smiling wryly, 'women are a

devilish complication in life.' He took her cup and set it down, then slid his arm around her. He brushed the lacy collar of her peignoir aside so that he could kiss her throat.

'Camille, you could drive any man crazy.' He pressed his lips to the juncture of her neck and shoulder, inhaling her fragrance. His hands gently caressed the soft flesh of her back.

'Antoine,' she gasped as he drew slightly back, 'this is crazy.' She was burning, her whole body quivering with excitement. 'It won't work. I want to be loved—I *must* be loved—by the man I give myself to.' She hoped he hadn't seen her deep, instinctive response to him, her agonising love for him.

'I think I'm going out of my mind,' he said thickly. 'Ah, Camille, you're so bewitching . . .'

His mouth moved over hers, warmly and seductively, so that she could not help responding. Her mouth opened involuntarily. She arched her neck, turning her face up to him, and her fingers somehow found their way to his hair. With a soft groan, he slid his fingers under her robe, seeking the soft smooth curve of her breasts, cupping them, teasing the nipples.

Camille found it almost impossible to resist the flames coursing through her body under his caresses. 'Antoine, please!' she said weakly, summoning up one last plea, and taking her hands from his hair before she lost control altogether. He pulled back at once, and she didn't know whether she was happy or sad to see him react so quickly.

Gently, he traced the outline of her lips with his fingertip. 'I'm sorry, Camille; I'm afraid I'm only flesh and blood.' He shrugged his broad shoulders and said quietly, 'Perhaps we'd better have all our talks in public places from now on.'

Reality came flooding back. The tide of emotion ebbed, and she was cold again, and empty.

Antoine stood up. 'You win. I'll tell Rémi to let you make yourself useful. If I give in gracefully, at least I can keep tabs on you.' He shook his head in exasperation, but his eyes were smiling gently.

As Camille watched him leave, she wondered why she didn't feel like celebrating. After all, she had just won the war.

CHAPTER FIVE

THE storm passed by mid-morning, and only a few tons of grapes developed bunch rot during the next critical few days; the gruelling work had paid off. The loss was unfortunate, of course, but not big enough to cast a pall over the coming harvest festivities.

In every village and estate along the Côte-d'Or there was excitement in the air. The new wine had finished its initial fermentation in the huge vats and had been poured into oak casks, where the process was being completed. The Burgundians, an ancient people who have perfected all that is best in eating and drinking—and know it—turned to other serious business: cooking, baking, sewing, and decorating for the coming celebrations.

The day after the final crushing dawned beautifully. Camille had overslept. Confident that Antoine had already left, she asked Joséphine to serve her breakfast on the private balcony that adjoined her suite and Antoine's.

She was just buttering her croissant when she heard Antoine's door open. Camille looked up, her heart leaping, to see Antoine's tall figure, dressed in casual work clothes, stroll on to the balcony.

Startled to see her there, he ran a hand through his thick black hair, still ruffled and disordered from sleep.

'*Bonjour*, Camille. What a lovely idea,' he said,

taking in the scene and the informality of her attire.

'It's such a beautiful day,' said Camille awkwardly, self-consciously aware of the way he was eyeing her figure through the fine cambric material of her pale turquoise lounge dress. Somehow, having Antoine see her in the early morning with her hair still damp from a shampoo, and with no make-up, set up that feeling of intimacy she had been fighting to avoid since the night of the storm, when she had almost given herself to him.

'May I join you?' The absence of the sardonic tone she had come to expect was disconcerting. Instead, his voice was warm, with a caressing quality about it that reminded her sharply of that night.

'Of course,' she responded faintly, only partly successful at hiding her alarm. 'I thought you had already gone down.'

'Overslept,' Antoine said, grinning, his brown eyes dancing in amusement.

He disappeared and then returned with his breakfast tray. Perched at one end was a small box of gilt-edged note cards and what looked like a long list of names.

'I just finished revising the guest list.' He sat down and poured himself a cup of coffee.

'Guest list?' echoed Camille, looking perplexedly at the welter of names.

Antoine smiled wryly. 'An old tradition at Château Villon. We invite our friends and few remaining relatives to help celebrate the new harvest.' He paused to sip his coffee. 'Of course, it's a little hectic to have so many house guests for four days, but it makes things very festive. And now that there is a new mistress at Château Villon . . .' his eyes travelled up and down her figure '. . . a delectable-looking one, even in the early morning, I can turn over the tedious task of issuing the invitations to her.'

'All these people descend for four days?' exclaimed Camille, deliberately ignoring his compliment. She wished he wouldn't keep moving his eyes over her. They were so obviously the eyes of a man who has always obtained what he wanted from women, and obtained it when he decided he wanted it.

'Yes, and most bring at least one servant. Then there is the first evening's buffet, when we also invite our neighbours.'

'I must confess, Antoine, I've never had any experience entertaining.' She hesitated, then added frankly, 'Unless you want to count the time the senior class picnic was held in my back yard.'

Antoine chuckled. 'It's amazing, Camille!'

'What's amazing?' she asked, piqued.

He put down his coffee cup, firmly picked up her hand and kissed the back of it. Her breathing stilled for a second as she trembled slightly at his touch.

'I wasn't laughing at you, *ma chérie*. Quite the opposite. I'm just amazed that you're so disarmingly honest about your background. One would think that once you found out that you were the granddaughter of one of the wealthiest men in all of France, you'd hide it or put on airs.'

Too conscious of his touch, she disengaged her hand. 'It's my father that's amazing, not me,' Camille said quietly, relieved that she had misjudged him. 'It would have been so easy for him to make me discontented with our life by telling me about Château Villon and the kind of life he used to lead. I'm grateful that he hid it from me, so that I had

a normal, average childhood,' she said sincerely.
'After all,' she added, smiling ruefully, 'he had no
idea his father had been nursing such a devious
scheme all these years to bring me here.'

'Your father must be remarkable,' Antoine said. 'I
was very young when he left France, only nine or ten,
so I barely remember him.'

'He is,' she agreed, pleased to hear respect in
Antoine's tone. 'You didn't live here then, did you?'

He shook his head as he poured them another cup
of coffee, and ate a bite of his croissant. 'No, my
mother and I lived in Paris then. I still have the
house. My father had died when I was just an infant, and my mother was your grandparents' only
niece, you know, and very close to them. It was
quite natural that when she died a few years later,
your grandfather became my guardian and I his
heir.'

'Yes, it would have been.'

Camille glanced out over the vineyards and valley
below and pictured Antoine as a boy of twelve or
thirteen coming here to live. And having been told all
these years that Château Villon would be his some
day, it was no surprise that he would fight to keep it.
Anyone would. Anyone, that is, but her romantic,
chivalrous father. Camille knew deep down she was
an impractical romantic too, just like Jean Adrien,
and love would always come first with her. But at the
same time she respected Antoine's sense of family
continuity. If only one could have both! But life often
just didn't turn out that way.

'Speaking of naturalness,' said Antoine, his voice
bringing her back to the present, 'don't worry about
the guests. You'll be a splendid hostess. Actually, too

natural and too attractive for my peace of mind.' He grinned engagingly. 'More and more, I wonder if I shouldn't just grab you by the hair and drag you off to my den whether you want to come or not.'

'You'd have to carry me off kicking and screaming,' she retorted primly. 'A relationship based on sheer physical attraction is not my ideal.'

'Women and their conventionalisms.' He pulled a wry face. 'Don't you want to cast off your virginal state and sample the most marvellous pleasures life has to offer?'

She bridled at his game-playing. 'What makes you so sure I'm a virgin?' Things were going to be increasingly difficult with this constant flicker of sexual awareness between them.

Antoine burst out laughing. 'I can tell.'

Her blush gave her away, but she ignored it. 'And I suppose you're going to tell me that women should sample these marvellous pleasures as freely as men do, and that if I don't it will be to my everlasting regret.'

'No, *ma petite.* I am not that selfish.' He was suddenly thoughtful, no longer teasing. 'That is why I let you escape from my arms the night of the storm. Now, if I were your *real* husband,' he said, smiling faintly, 'I would claim the privilege of being my wife's first and last lover.'

Camille sat very still and listened to his words with a sinking heart. What Antoine was saying was that she was safe with him. There was no doubt that his intention of divorcing her hadn't wavered in the slightest, but he was telling her that, out of respect for her, he intended to leave her innocent for a 'real' husband in the future.

As soon as he finished speaking, Antoine drank the last of his coffee. 'Well, I'd better be getting on. You'll find that Madame Gounod and Henri will be pleased to assist you with all the preparations,' he added in a preoccupied voice, his mind already on the day's work ahead.

Camille managed to maintain a calm exterior and to murmur something conventional as he left. Decisively, she made an effort to pull herself together. She was jumping to conclusions too quickly, she told herself stoutly. Just because he didn't show any signs of falling in love with her yet, that wasn't to say he wouldn't in time.

Somewhat heartened, she picked up the guest list. As she glanced at it, her eyes fell on one name, halfway down. Jusserand. Camille felt herself growing cold again. Antoine must be inviting her for only one reason, she thought in agony, as tears sprang to her eyes. He knew Camille had fallen in love with him, and he meant this to be a subtle but effective warning. How could he be so cruel? Why couldn't he just tell her she hadn't a chance with him, instead of forcing her to go through four days of hell to make his point?

Getting ready for the guests took an amazing amount of time. Decisions had to be made about rooms, entertainments, menus. Any spare minutes, with the exception of her daily half-hour chess games with her grandfather, had to be spent learning folk dances. She and Antoine were to open the estate workers' festival by dancing the first ones in old folk costumes. Later in the evening, they and their house guests would change into more formal attire and attend the exclusive harvest ball, this year hosted by François and Hélène Chevillot.

Joséphine was spending her spare moments altering the beautiful old costume that Madame Deslandes had worn, to fit her granddaughter. When she could, she helped Camille with some of the dance steps, a chore more to her liking.

'No, *madame*, that's not right,' chided Joséphine, giggling, as she watched Camille go through the particularly complex *allemande* that would begin the festivities. 'You started off on your right foot instead of your left and now it is hopeless.'

'That's not the problem, Joséphine,' sighed Camille, sinking into a chair. 'The problem is that I seem to have two *left* feet today.'

Her maid's face clouded in concern. 'You aren't feeling unwell, are you?' she asked. 'The guests are arriving tonight and the festival is tomorrow. How awful if you took sick!'

'No, I'm not sick,' said Camille reassuringly. 'Perhaps I'm just nervous about all the responsibility.' Secretly she knew it wasn't that either; it was the knowledge that tonight Eugénie Jusserand would be there, at Château Villon. She dreaded the agony of watching her with Antoine, perhaps even seeing them slip away to be alone. Did she have the fortitude to stand by without making a fool of herself?

'I think I'll rest before lunch,' she said. 'Tomorrow morning we can have one more practice session, and I promise to concentrate.' She smiled softly. 'I won't embarrass you at the festival.'

'Oh, *madame*,' cried Joséphine, 'you could never embarrass me! You'll look so beautiful no one will even notice how you are dancing.'

At noon, with Antoine in Beaune on wine business, she lunched with her grandfather on the terrace. She enjoyed the unusually light repast that had been prepared. The cook was busy with preparations for the evening buffet, and had made them no more than a simple quiche and salad, served with fresh bread, cheese, and fruit. Usually the big meal of the day was served at this time, a custom Camille found difficult to adjust to. She was still American enough to prefer it in the evening, as a kind of reward for having finished the day's work.

After lunch the two of them resumed a chess game started the day before in Monsieur Deslandes's study. The old man seemed to relish these battles of wit with his granddaughter, and Camille made sure nothing interfered with their times together, always so short because of how easily he tired.

'That was an unfortunate move,' he said sternly, shifting his knight to catch Camille's queen and rook in a fork. 'You don't seem yourself today, *ma petite*. What is bothering you?'

'Nothing really . . . the excitement, I guess,' she answered, moving her queen out of reach of the knight, and enjoying the relish with which he captured her rook.

Her grandfather's eyebrows rose as he eyed her intently. 'Excitement, or the imminent arrival of Mademoiselle Jusserand?'

Camille felt her cheeks grow warm. Disconcerted, she quickly moved her own bishop and captured his knight. A knight for a rook was a poor trade, but better than nothing at all. 'I don't know what you mean, *Grand-père* . . . It's your move.'

'No, of course you don't. Nor has it occurred to

you how insensitive it is of Antoine to invite her, considering the . . . arrangement between you two.' He moved a bishop, again threatening her queen.

'Arrangement?' she pretended nonchalance, but her stomach knotted. She moved her queen out of harm's way with trembling fingers.

With a flourish, he ruthlessly captured her queen with a cunningly shielded knight. Then he raised his head to look her squarely in the eyes.

'You know what arrangement I mean,' he said dryly. 'I imagine it runs along the lines of, "Let's go along with dear old *Grand-père*. He doesn't have much time left, and it will make him happy." Am I right?'

Camille couldn't think of anything to say.

'Then, after I have passed on—happy to the end— there will be a sensible, tidy divorce to make things right. *Très moderne.*'

Camille could hear her heart pounding. 'How did you know?' she asked quietly, gazing wide-eyed at him.

Charles Deslandes chuckled. 'Your move.'

Camille glanced back at the board and tried to focus on the pieces. She moved a pawn randomly.

'I may not be able to leave my room much these days,' he said, 'but I have ways of finding out the things that go on; things such as the mistress of the estate working in the fields.' He glared at her, but without conviction. She could, in fact, see respect in his eyes. 'Besides, you two gave in far too easily.'

'But—'

'Moreover,' he continued, ignoring her interruption, 'I can read Antoine like a book. And as for you, your face is so transparent you couldn't pull the wool over the eyes of a newborn lamb.'

'We didn't mean to hurt you, *Grand-père*, but you did put us in a ridiculous situation,' she said lamely.

'Oh, I was expecting something like this,' he said airily.

'Then you aren't angry with us?' Camille exclaimed, relief flooding through her. She had grown too fond of the outrageous old devil to want to see him hurt.

'I'm not dead and buried yet, and I still have a trick or two up my sleeve,' he responded, compelling Camille's king into a dangerous corner with his rook. 'You have fallen in love with Antoine, just as I predicted, haven't you?'

Camille blushed in confusion. 'I haven't—'

'Don't bother to deny it, *ma chérie*; it's written all over your face. Your face also tells me that you can't understand how Antoine could be so heartless as to have Eugénie visit while you are forced to go through with this charade, as you no doubt refer to it.'

'Perhaps he suspects I've fallen in love with him and it's his way of warning me off,' she informed him, misery clearly visible in her face.

Charles Deslandes reached over and patted her hand comfortingly. 'Antoine had removed the Jusserands from the list this year. It was I who insisted they come.'

Camille gazed at him in surprise. 'You! I don't understand!' Her heart missed a beat as a sudden flame of hope flickered inside her.

Her grandfather shrugged expressively. 'Antoine is a blockhead when it comes to women. I can tell he's attracted to you, but until he takes Eugénie

Jusserand off her pedestal and sees her as the super-ficial ninny she is, he'll never appreciate the prize he has in his own lap.'

'Why do you think having her here will make any difference?'

'He will be forced to compare the two of you together. And with a woman like her, once she is seen clearly, familiarity breeds contempt. An old French expression.'

'We say it in America, too, *Grand-père*,' Camille admonished, 'but we also say one shouldn't put the fox in with the chickens. How do you know he won't be more attracted to her rather than less? People aren't pawns, you know,' she said, not hiding her vexation as she moved her remaining bishop closer to her king to protect it.

The sparkle went from his eyes. 'I learned that lesson years ago,' he said sadly. 'I suppose you told Jean Adrien about your little arrangement, and that is why he has not been threatening me with physical violence unless I release his daughter.' He looked askance at Camille and read the truth on her face. 'I thought so.'

Remorseful, Camille moved around the table and knelt to throw her arms around him. 'You are an absolute rogue . . . and you haven't learned your lesson or you'd never have dreamed up this imposs-ible marriage. But I've grown to love you, anyway,' she said shyly, then added softly: 'Antoine, too.' She drew back and looked at him imploringly. 'But you have to promise me something, *Grand-père*, on your honour. Please, please don't force Antoine to stay with me after you're gone. Don't put some clause in your will or . . . or anything. Let him decide on his own whom he loves. I won't—can't live my life with a man who doesn't love me as much as I love him.'

He smiled down at her. 'Never fear that, *ma petite*. I decided long ago that if Antoine doesn't have the brains to choose you on his own, he doesn't deserve you.' The sparkle returned to his old eyes. 'But I can give him a little push in the right direction, can't I?'

'You're terrible, do you know that?' she said, hugging him again.

'Don't try to soften me up,' he said sternly, but as if to belie his words, his old arms tightened around her affectionately.

'Soften you up?' Puzzled, Camille drew back.

'I will have you in checkmate on the next move.'

Camille quickly scanned the board. His queen had a clear field to drop down next to her king, with his rook to protect it. There was nothing she could do to prevent it.

'Just you wait until tomorrow's game,' she threatened. 'I'll win yet.'

He smiled. 'I never doubted it.'

Charles Deslandes, ageless and patrician in a flawlessly cut evening jacket, every inch the *seigneur* of the manor, joined Camille and Antoine to greet the arriving guests. Drawing comfort from his presence at her side, she met them with more aplomb than she had thought possible—even the Jusserand family, who arrived last.

Monsieur Jusserand was a heavyset, jovial man who greeted Camille with warmth. His wife, not in the least jovial, was a chic, silver-haired woman, from whom Eugénie had obviously received her looks and her hauteur.

'Good evening,' she said in English, through compressed lips. It was much the way a San Francisco matron might greet a taxi-cab driver.

Camille, friendly but warily aloof, shook Madame Jusserand's limp, cold hand, and turned her head to smile pleasantly at Eugénie and Edouard, who followed their parents up the stairs. Eugénie, sleek and ultra-elegant, languidly murmured a few conventional words of greeting. As Camille responded politely, Charles Deslandes moved closer to her and casually draped an arm around her shoulders, a subtle signal—for which Camille could have kissed him—that Eugénie faced formidable opposition in any attempt to undercut Camille's position.

'It's good to see you, Eugénie, looking marvellous, as always,' he said dryly, giving her an amused, oblique smile, and then included her brother in his glance. 'And you, too, Edouard. It will be nice for our newly-weds to have some young people in the house, instead of just us old fogies, eh, Jusserand? I refer of course, to *monsieur*, not *madame*.'

Madame smiled a cold, thin smile which made no pretence at warmth, but Monsieur Jusserand laughed heartily, clapping his old friend on the back. Eugénie's face was frozen, masklike, and Edouard, as usual, looked distantly amused.

As the party moved into the drawing room to join the other guests, Antoine greeted Eugénie with an amiable kiss on the cheek, and then spoke to her in low, friendly tones. Despite Camille's outward composure, the sight gave her a shaky, sinking feeling. It was small comfort to know he greeted all the female guests that way. Realising that the next four days were going to be the hardest she had ever faced, she took a deep breath. She wished she was as confident as her grandfather about the outcome. With gratitude, she accepted a glass of champagne from Henri, who was circulating with a full tray.

Charles Deslandes and Monsieur Jusserand at once sought out the nearest discussion on the new wine, and they didn't have far to go. Crop damage from the rain was the topic of almost all the conversations in the room.

To her surprise, Camille found herself quickly the centre of a covey of males, both young and old, all eager for her attention and asking her—strange subject for a group of Frenchmen around a pretty girl—about the grape harvest at Château Villon. Although she knew she was attractive in her simple, classic white cocktail dress with its intricately embroidered cummerbund—of grapes and vines, in tribute to the season, naturally—she was puzzled by the serious, fervent attention. When they moved towards the buffet tables, Edouard deftly but firmly grasped her elbow, drawing her away.

'I've been circling that wolf-pack for half an hour trying to get a foot in,' he said mournfully, in the husky, seductive tone that he habitually used with women. 'Why they should find it so admirable that you've been grubbing about the vines as industriously as poor old Antoine, I'll never know.'

'People are talking about that?' asked Camille, blushing in distress. 'That explains all the attention I've been getting. Antoine must be mortified. I'm afraid I laughed at him when he said it would be an embarrassment.'

'An embarrassment!' scoffed Edouard. 'He has

the admiration of the entire male population of the Côte-d'Or; not only a wife as beautiful as Venus, but as strong and determined as Jeanne d'Arc.'

'Really, Edouard, you're exaggerating, as usual,' admonished Camille, flustered, 'but tell me seriously: my working in the fields that night doesn't reflect badly on Antoine?'

'Are you joking? I heard one man suggest sending a delegation to the Napa Valley to select wives for their unmarried sons!'

Camille laughed in relief. 'I hope you aren't making this up to make me feel better.'

'Cross my heart.' said Edouard solemnly.

Later, after the buffet, Hélène Chevillot further set Camille's mind at ease.

'I should be angry with you,' she said. 'Either I'm going to have to threaten François with divorce or learn to pick grapes myself to get his attention back. He's been singing your praises for days.'

Camille had to laugh at the thought of the delicate Hélène in work clothes. 'Honestly, Hélène, I didn't mean to create a sensation. It was a very natural thing for me to do. At home, no one would have thought anything about it.'

Hélène shook her head in amusement. 'Nevertheless, expect to see a few jealous daggers glinting in female eyes for a while. Ah, I can see your handsome husband heading determinedly in this direction. I'm sure you'd like a second alone,' she said, smiling, then drifted away.

Camille stood glued to the spot, afraid to turn. Unsure of how a man like Antoine would take all the conversation—admiring or not—about his wife, she had been carefully avoiding him.

Feeling his masculine hands grip her shoulders from behind, her heart stopped.

'*Ma femme*,' said Antoine gently, turning her around.

Her heart beat wildly at the words as she gazed into his dark eyes. *Femme*: literal translation, *woman*. But in conventional French, *ma femme* meant not *my woman*, but *my wife*. He had never said it to her before.

He smiled and clasped his arm possessively around her waist. She could feel the warm, confident pressure of his fingers just below the swell of her breasts.

'I think we'd best start shepherding our guests home or up to their rooms, don't you?' he asked cheerfully, smiling down at her. 'It's going to be an awfully long day tomorrow.' The inflection of voice, his gaze, everything about him, made it seem as if he were in fact what he appeared to be in public—a happy, newly married man, enamoured with his young wife.

Dressing for bed that night, she wondered what Antoine, just a few short steps and a door away, was thinking. *Did* he mean anything when he called her *ma femme*? How would he respond if she were to knock on his door? It would be so easy, and there would be no question about what would happen if she did. But if things didn't turn out the way she hoped and dreamed they would, then wouldn't she find herself involved in nothing more than a temporary physical relationship? Could she settle for that?

No, she decided, facing the thought squarely, she could not. It would be impossible for her to retain her pride and dignity—let alone her self-respect, as old-fashioned as that sounded—in such a situation. It had to be all or nothing. With that bleak realisation, she slipped between the sheets and stared blankly at the ceiling, trying to still the hunger for him that burned through her veins.

CHAPTER SIX

SHE was awakened early from a restless sleep by the sounds of hammering in the courtyard below. Drawing on a robe she stepped out on to the terrace and looked down on a scene of surprising activity. Several workers were festooning the gilded railings with wreaths of grape leaves and flowers. Others were wrestling beautifully carved oak barrels of wine on to sturdy trestle tables. The hammering was coming from the far corner, where a few men were knocking together some more trestle tables, no doubt for food. Waving briefly at one of the workmen who caught sight of her, grinned, and doffed his hat, she quickly retreated inside.

There was a great deal to be done before the festival began at noon, and the morning raced by in a whirl of activity, leaving Camille anxious and unsure of her role in the celebration.

'Joséphine,' Camille cried, 'do you have to lace it so tightly?'

'One more inch, *madame*,' said Joséphine, relentlessly pulling on the laces.

'Another *inch*?' she gasped. 'I won't breathe.'

Ruthlessly, the maid tugged once more at the strategic instant of Camille's gasp. Securing the lacing tightly she stepped back and smiled broadly at her work. '*Voilà!* The figure of an hourglass, just like your *grand'mère*, except that you are more ...'

Joséphine paused, searching for words '. . . woman-ly,' she said tentatively.

Camille looked dubiously into the mirror at her figure in full petticoats and old-fashioned, full-torso corset, and was shocked beyond her expectations. Her waist was incredibly dainty, it was true, but the corset had pushed her breasts up so high they looked like lush, ripe fruit about to spill completely out of their cups. '*Mon dieu!*' she cried in distress, 'the blouse was cut low enough when I tried it on without the corset!'

Joséphine did not actually say 'pooh-pooh', but her look implied it clearly enough. 'Don't worry, *madame*; there is a fringe of lace, remember.' She helped Camille draw on the delicate blouse and the full skirt of cambric embellished with embroidered floral borders. Then, with a cluck of satisfaction, she tied the lacy white apron around her waist.

Camille found Joséphine's comforting words hol-low. The narrow strip of lace did nothing except make her breasts look more naked than ever. She remembered paintings of French peasant scenes that she had seen at the de Young Museum in San Francisco on a high school field trip. The girls, Camille included, had giggled at the sight of the rosy-cheeked, smiling maidens in the pictures, danc-ing merrily with equally rosy breasts completely revealed. Now she knew where the artists had got their inspiration. If she didn't watch how she moved, she would be very completely revealed herself. This would be an afternoon when erect posture was an absolute requirement.

Adjusting a wreath of flowers on Camille's up-swept curls, Joséphine stepped back to inspect her creation critically. '*C'est parfait,*' she sighed. 'Now I must go and quickly change, too. I must see Monsieur Antoine and you when you make your entrance.'

She left the room and closed the door behind her, then opened it again and popped her head in. 'Remember, left foot first!'

Camille was vainly trying to adjust the bodice of her blouse to a more seemly height when Antoine knocked and called to her from the hallway. 'Camille, are you ready? It's late.'

'I don't know,' she answered weakly.

'What do you mean, you don't know?' he asked, opening her door. He walked in, looking at his watch, then halted, his breath drawn in audibly. 'You look fantastic . . . like a Renoir painting!' he said.

'Antoine, I can't wear this!' Camille wailed. 'It must have been designed when the French held orgies, not dances! I can't believe my grandmother ever wore this!'

Antoine laughed. 'She did, all right, but she never looked like that!' His eyes sparkled as he stared hungrily at her breasts. 'She didn't have . . . have . . .' He cupped his hands expressively in the timeless gesture of men everywhere, then placed them lightly around her waist. 'I suppose we did have orgies once upon a time, and I'm not letting you out of my sight, just in case any amorous types start thinking along those lines again.'

Without giving her a chance to reply, he pulled her out of the room and into the corridor. Her heart failing, Camille forced herself to stand erect and to look casual as they descended the stairs. She drew strength from her own growing sense of self-possession, and from her increasing understanding of the French way of looking at things: sensual earthy, and pragmatic. Only if she revealed her own embarrassment at the shocking *décolletage* of her costume would people think about it. Stares, however, she would have to bear.

The sounds of voices and laughter from the drawing room drifted up, but most of the men stopped and stared at Camille in open admiration when she entered with Antoine.

'I know that look,' he whispered in her ear. 'They are thinking how ripe you look for the picking, and'—he kissed her ear gently—'how they wish they were the one with the right to harvest.'

Eugénie was standing near the fireplace and her catlike eyes stared at Camille in open enmity. Like the rest of the guests, she was also in costume, but unfortunately for her, the peasant style didn't suit her svelte, twentieth-century figure.

Antoine, looking quite rakish in white pantaloons, brightly coloured knee socks, and an elaborately embroidered shirt, affected a bland air, but she could tell he was enjoying the expressions on the guest's faces.

'You're wonderful,' he said, again speaking for her ear alone. 'I'm proud to have you at my side.'

Beaming at the sight of her, Charles Deslandes dropped a kiss on his granddaughter's cheek and shooed the guests out the door and into the courtyard to begin the festival.

The courtyard was crowded with estate workers and their families, also dressed in the old costumes. As Camille stepped outside, a boy bearing a huge bouquet of flowers was thrust out of the crowd and approached her shyly, head hanging down.

'*Merci beaucoup*,' said Camille, accepting the flowers.

'*De rien*, Madame de Breze,' he recited almost inaudibly, staring at his feet.

At once she recognised him, and smiled. '*Comment ça va, mon ami Jules?*'

His head came up and he grinned. '*Très bien, merci, madame*,' he said delightedly.

Monsieur Deslandes raised his hand, and a man standing ready with a mallet knocked the bung from the first barrel of new wine. The wine poured out in a purple stream, everyone cheered, and the festival was underway. Ceremoniously, Rémi Fouquet filled a silver goblet under the tap. Then with shouts of laughter, the crowd surged forward to fill their mugs and glasses.

Rémi handed the goblet to Charles Deslandes who gave the first toast, then to Antoine who gave the second.

Exercising the traditional privilege of estate manager, Rémi took hold of Camille's arm, while his wife, a cheerful, plump matron, grabbed Antoine's. The four formed a circle, and the musicans started to play, softly and slowly.

'Left foot, left foot,' Camille said to herself, and to her relief, she started correctly. As the music picked up in tempo and sound, she found herself enjoying the exhilaration of the dance. Once they had moved through the first round, Rémi released her hand and opened wide the circle for others to join in.

Camille lost track of the time as they alternately danced to the music, sipped wine, and nibbled food from the heavily loaded trestle tables: succulent roasted meats, casseroles, breads, pungent cheeses, fruits, and cakes and tarts almost too beautiful to be eaten. Almost, but not quite.

At dusk everyone retreated to rest and change for the evening ball at the Chevillots'. Camille made sure her grandfather was settled for the evening.

'You've had a hard day, *Grand-père*. You should go to bed early tonight.'

'Early? I was thinking of joining the rest of you at the ball,' he said innocently.

'You just try it,' she said, 'and you'll have me to contend with. I want your lights out by nine. And remember, I have my spies, too.'

'Little did I know I was bringing a tyrant into the house,' he muttered as she kissed him goodnight, but then he added, 'I have not had such a happy afternoon in many years. You were pretty as a picture, *ma chérie*. I wish your old *grand'mère* had lived to see you. But then, he added with a smile, 'what would *she* have worn?'

Retreating to her own room, she twirled herself about, humming to the music still wafting up from below, and feeling exquisitely happy. She didn't even attempt to quell the thought that kept running through her mind—Antoine was falling in love with her. She was sure she could read the signs all afternoon: the caressing glances, the possessive hovering nearby, the cutting in when he felt a man had danced with her long enough. Especially Edouard, she noted with amusement. And most important of all, he had positively ignored Eugénie.

Impulsively, she went to the closet and took out the green gown she had worn the night of their engagement. Then she opened the grey silk box with the Deslandes emeralds. She looked at them for a long time, struck with the strange feeling that they had lain there, lustrous and darkly opalescent, somehow waiting for her to put them on again. '*Merci, grand'mère,*' she whispered.

The limousines were waiting for them at nine, but they were at the rear entrance instead of the front, because the party was still in full swing in the courtyard. Antoine didn't comment on Camille's choice of dress, but he raised an eyebrow and smiled. Even the Jusserands' sharing of their car failed to affect Camille's happiness.

At the Chevillots' château there were people everywhere, spilling out of the ballroom and on to the moonlit terrace. Several people called out greetings to Antoine and Camille, and she glowed; they were, it was clear, an established pair. After greeting François and Hélène, Antoine drew Camille in among the dancing couples in the ballroom without a backward glance at Eugénie. There was laughter in his brillant eyes as he pulled her closer.

'I can't help marvelling at the impact you've made in the valley, on your grandfather . . . and on me, in such a short time, *ma chérie*,' he murmured in her ear, brushing it lightly with his lips. He lingered there a moment longer than necessary, and Camille knew he was inhaling the fragrance of her hair.

Too happy for words, she clung to him as they danced, her whole body yielding and melting at the touch of his lean, hard frame.

Halfway through the dance, François Chevillot expertly cut in. 'You've monopolised her long enough, Antoine. As a responsible host I must see to it everyone gets a chance to dance with this enchanting creature.'

'You first, of course,' retorted Antoine, smiling.

'Of course.'

From then on she found herself dancing with a succession of attentive, courteous men who showered her with the wildly exaggerated Gallic compliments at which the French are so notably adept. Camille gave in to the mood of the evening and thoroughly enjoyed herself.

After an hour, though, longing for another dance with Antoine, she began looking for him over the shoulders of her partners. When she thought she caught a glimpse of him going out through the terrace doors, she excused herself and followed him. Stepping out into the cool, fragrant night air, she was at once the object of several pairs of male eyes, but she didn't see Antoine's among them.

Had he gone for a stroll? It was stuffy in the ballroom, and the air out here was fresh, the stars bright and cold. A stroll in the formal garden wasn't a bad idea, she thought. It would give her a chance to catch her breath. And perhaps she would cross Antoine's path.

Walking along the meandering gravel path, savouring the quiet and the scent of the flowers, Camille spied a floodlit fountain, its water jets sparkling like strings of iridescent jewels. She moved towards it, so charmed by the soft splashing sounds, and by the water cascading gently down upon a beautiful bronze water nymph, that she didn't see the couple locked in an embrace until she was almost upon them. They moved quickly apart. Bewildered, Camille found herself staring at a disconcerted

Antoine and a coldly smiling Eugénie. Eugénie had left a bejewelled hand possessively on his arm as she turned.

'I didn't mean to . . .' Camille's voice failed her, and she fled.

To her surprise, Antoine followed her, pulling her to an abrupt halt before she was halfway to the terrace. He turned her around to face him.

'Camille, let me explain—' he began.

She cut him off impatiently. 'You don't need to explain!' Her luminous, tear-filled eyes flashed. 'It was obvious enough what you were doing, and what you do in private is your own business. Our marriage *is* only a business arrangement, after all.'

He grasped her by her bare shoulders, and shook her. 'It wasn't what it seemed!'

Eugénie's seductive tones floated through the soft garden air. 'Antoine, where are you?'

'Let me go, or I'll make a scene,' Camille snapped, her voice brittle. She choked back the sobs welling up inside; she wouldn't cry in front of him!

Antoine swore and his face twisted in fury as she wrenched herself out of his hands and ran down the path.

'Camille!' she heard him call. 'Damn you! Camille!'

She sought the farthest reaches of the garden on the far side of the terrace, where there were few lights. There in the fragrant darkness she sank down on the marble bench and burst into tears. She lay sideways, putting her cheek against the cool, impersonal marble of the bench, seeing in her mind the awful scene again. How could she have acted like such a fool—baring her heart to both of them . . . practically trumpeting her love for Antoine? Oh,

God, that gloating sneer on Eugénie's face . . . ! She closed her eyes and slowly gained control over her emotions, then quietly sat up. She had to go back to the ballroom. It wouldn't do to have anyone coming out to look for her.

She slipped into the château by a side entrance, startling a young maid emerging from a pantry.

'Would *madame* care to use a guest room to freshen up?' the maid asked, looking at her with obvious concern.

Camille repaired the damage the tears had made to her make-up, and inspected her face carefully in the oval, ebony-framed mirror. Her skin was pale, but her green eyes sparkled more brilliantly than the jewels around her neck. Fortunately she hadn't cried long enough to turn them red. She would pass inspection, she decided.

She stood a while longer in front of the mirror. 'He doesn't love you,' she whispered to the reflection. 'Get that through your thick head. He never said he did, and he never will say it.' She closed her eyes and shuddered as a wave of despair washed over her. How was she going to survive until she could go back home to California where she belonged?

Entering the ballroom again, head held high, she ran immediately into Edouard.

'Where have you been?' he asked, swinging her expertly on to the dance floor. 'I haven't had a single dance with you all night.'

She forced herself to smile warmly at him. Perhaps what she needed, she thought, was someone like Edouard, someone attractive but unthreatening, to keep her mind off Antoine. 'I'll have to make it up to you,' she answered softly.

Edouard looked down at her, puzzled at the lack of banter he had come to expect. 'Pale cheeks,' he said, 'eyes even brighter than usual. You've been crying, and I suspect it has something to do with Eugénie and Antoine.'

'Is it that obvious?' she asked in despair.

'Don't worry,' Edouard said in a brotherly tone, although the way he pulled her closer was not entirely brotherly, 'you are in good hands. Consoling distraught females is my forte.'

She smiled at him gratefully. 'Perhaps I *have* been taking life a bit too seriously. I think I need to relax a little.'

'Then I'm your man,' he murmured softly into her ear.

Several dances later, with Edouard having monopolised her for most of them, she encountered Antoine's lancing eyes. It couldn't have been plainer that he had been watching her. Edouard did his level best to keep them out of his way, but gave her away gracefully when Antoine finally cut in. Antoine was less graceful. Without a word to Edouard, he whirled her away, holding her at a very proper distance.

'Haven't you danced enough with that Don Juan for one night?' he asked curtly.

'I don't know why that's any concern of yours,' said Camille, pretending nonchalance, while her heart beat furiously at his nearness. Damn, she thought, it didn't seem fair that he could make her feel this way against her will. 'He's a very good dancer, and I enjoy his company.'

'I couldn't fail to notice that,' he muttered grimly. 'His company isn't suitable for you. He's a philanderer; he hasn't worked a day in his life. If the family weren't old friends I wouldn't put up with him.'

'I don't see what business it is of yours if I choose to amuse myself with Edouard. I'm not one of your possessions, you know,' she said coldly. 'I like him very much and I intend to spend as much time with him as I want.' She paused, then added, 'I never have believed much in a double standard.'

'Double standard?' asked Antoine angrily.

'Yes, and I must apologise for my little scene in the garden,' Camille said, affecting a bored tone. 'You have a perfect right to have your own friends, just as I do.'

Antoine's eyes flashed, then turned flinty. 'Certainly,' he said sarcastically, 'but of course we must be properly discreet about it.'

'Of course,' she said tauntingly, 'one must keep up appearances.'

His mouth became a hard, fierce line. 'If that's the way you want it.'

'That's the way I want it,' she answered flatly.

'A dance floor is not the place to discuss this, I think,' he answered through clenched teeth.

'It seems to me we've said all there is to say. Now, if you will excuse me, I'm really too tired to dance any longer.'

She could feel his smouldering gaze on her back as she walked away. Within her, her heart was like lead.

Antoine followed her into her sitting room that night, resolutely shoving the door open and entering when she tried to shut it in his face.

'I mean to talk to you,' he said grimly, 'and I'm going to stay here all night if that's what it takes to get you to listen.'

'Suit yourself!' she snapped. 'The settee's too short for you, but you're welcome to it.' She walked to the bureau and took off her emeralds.

He followed her, picking them up from where she dropped them. 'For a moment this evening,' he said slowly, looking at the necklace in his hand, 'when I saw you wearing these, I thought you were . . . telling me something.' His hand clenched the gleaming jewels.

'I don't know what you mean,' Camille said calmly, her heart fluttering. She started to leave for the bedroom, but Antoine lashed out and grabbed her by the wrist.

'I didn't arrange to meet Eugénie in the garden. I stumbled across her when I was out for some fresh air,' he said hoarsely. 'She was upset; she felt our marriage was no longer just a business arrangement . . . and she accused me of falling in love with you.'

'So the kiss was to convince her how wrong she was?' said Camille in arched tones. 'I don't see why I have to listen to this.' She tried to free her wrist. 'Please let me go.'

'No, I . . . I told her I didn't know if I was falling in love with you or not, but I knew I couldn't honestly say I wanted to divorce you as soon as possible after all.' Antoine stared down at Camille, his eyes full of emotion, but impossible to read. 'She started to cry . . . I was comforting her and—all right, it turned into a kiss.'

'And you expect me to believe you really didn't mean it, I suppose, and you certainly didn't enjoy it!'

Antoine took a long, deep breath. 'There really isn't any point in this, is there? I thought you were grown up, Camille, and knew what you wanted out of life, but I was wrong, I see. You're not ready to fight for what you want. You're ready to give it up because you didn't get it the moment you wanted it.'

He let go of her wrist. Turning, he strode away, then turned again at the door to say something, but thought better of it. The door closed sharply behind him, leaving Camille standing in the middle of the room, sick and forlorn.

Some of what he'd said was true; the childish way she'd run, her refusal to listen to explanations. But was it really true that he was falling in love with her? That he wanted to remain married to her?

Her heart beat agitatedly as she paced the room, hearing his words over and over, wanting to believe them, knowing that only pride was stopping her from going to him right then.

A sudden new thought struck like a dagger into her heart. Perhaps he wanted to stay married, but not for the reason she hoped. Antoine didn't know that *Grand-père* had agreed not to tie the inheritance to the continuation of the marriage. Was it possible that he had begun to fear such a clause in Monsieur Deslandes's will—or, with Gallic fatalism, to expect it? Certainly, he had seen her grandfather's growing attachment to her, and he must have noticed her popularity with the estate workers. After all, hadn't he expressed surprise only a few hours ago at how quickly she had established a place for herself?

So perhaps he had decided the most sensible thing for him to do was to resign himself to things as they were; to feign his love and consummate their marriage, and thereby ensure his right to the estate. He was the sort of man, Camille thought, to whom Château Villon might be more important than any woman. After Charles Deslandes died, he could always take a mistress to provide the missing ingredient in his marriage. Camille had already learned many Frenchmen did just that.

She shivered. Could it really be possible? He was a superb actor; that she knew—able to turn emotions on and off like a tap. How could she risk believing that what he had said was the truth? Once she did that, once she let herself believe he was really beginning to love her, there would be no turning back. She would find herself trapped by her own unleashed passion into a loveless parody of marriage, grovelling for crumbs of affection.

Tortured with longing and with doubt she collapsed in tears on her bed. Heartsick, she realised she would never be able to reveal her own love to Antoine or to believe in his, until her dear grandfather's death.

Only then would Antoine's actions speak for themselves.

CHAPTER SEVEN

THE dew on the young vine leaves sparkled like tiny diamonds in the early-morning July sun. Camille was ruthlessly pruning many of the tender, green shoots, while her workers were tying branches to the wire trellises. The work was necessary to allow easy passage between the rows and to make sure that the new bunches of grapes faced the sun.

It seemed impossible, she thought, as she clipped mechanically away. Almost ten months had gone by since that awful night of the harvest ball. An impenetrable barrier had sprung up between her and Antoine, a barrier neither of them had attempted to dispel. As always, Antoine was polite and attentive to her in public. But in private they might as well have been living on different planets.

'*Bonjour!* I see you're at it again!' Rémi Fouquet's face broke into a lopsided grin. Over the months, Camille had gained his professional respect, but they disagreed over just how much the vines should be cut back while growing.

'Yes, I'm at it,' she said, smiling. She took off a heavy glove to wipe her forehead with the back of her hand.

'Prune, prune, that's all you do.' He shook his head sceptically. 'You'll have a better grape, *certainement*, but will there be enough wine to make a profit? You must think about that too, eh?'

'We'll see soon enough now, Rémi,' said Camille, hiding her amusement.

Rémi had said the same thing every week since the beginning of spring, when the vines, cut back and dormant through the winter, had started to grow again.

Last autumn, at her prompting, he had persuaded Antoine to let her have her own section of the lower vineyard to manage. Antoine had consented indifferently, but had made it clear that he himself would have nothing to do with the project or—by inference—with her. If her section didn't produce good grapes or failed to make a profit, the responsibility would be Rémi's.

With blind faith—more in his uncle Bernard's judgment than hers, Camille supposed—Rémi had magnanimously let her make all the decisions.

'No manual work, though; it would reflect badly on your position as Madame de Breze,' he had warned sternly when telling her about Antoine's decision. 'I'll assign you a crew and you can give all the orders.'

She had faithfully stuck to the agreement through the mild, long winter and the short spring. Under her direction the workers turned the soil, fertilised, banked earth against the trunks, and hoed. By early summer Antoine had grudgingly admitted to Rémi that her section was in perfect shape and doing well. But now was the time of the most critical pruning, and she was doing it herself, despite the ban on physical labour. She was convinced the slight drop in quality of the Villon grapes under Rémi's management was due to overly timid pruning, and she wanted to prove she was right.

'If you keep this up,' Rémi said nervously, 'we'll have the best vines in France. But no grapes.'

Rémi's apprehension must be increasing, she thought, slipping on the glove and continuing to work under his frown. He'd said the same thing three times in as many days.

'Just remember our wager,' she teased. 'I have every intention of ordering the most expensive dinner on the menu.'

'I don't know how you talked me into a bet,' he grumbled. 'I lose either way.'

'What do you mean?'

'If you're right, I have to buy you dinner. If I'm right, and there aren't enough grapes for a profit, I get a free dinner,' he said, 'but I lose my job.'

'Never!' she exclaimed, then added reassuringly, 'Antoine couldn't do without you. Besides, you could always come to work for us in America.'

Rémi looked only partially cheered. 'When do you want to spray against mildew?'

'Tomorrow would be fine,' she answered.

'Good.' He paused and his expression turned suddenly cross. 'It looks like you have a visitor. I'd best get back to work.' He turned and walked away without a further word.

Camille didn't have to look up to know it was Edouard. Rémi didn't like him at all, especially because Edouard's visits always coincided with Antoine's absences from the estate.

She watched Rémi leave, knowing he was unhappy and confused about Camille's relationship with Antoine. There was little she could say to comfort him, she thought bitterly, because she was far more unhappy than he.

She would long ago have begged her grandfather to let her go home, but his health had taken a serious turn for the worse, and she didn't have the heart to leave him. Charles Deslandes seldom left his rooms now, and although his mental faculties were still alert, his body was wasting away before her eyes. Each day he grew more heart-breakingly frail, more shrunken. Hiding her personal worries from him as well as she could, she had resolved to stay as long as he needed her.

Fortunately, she had her work. And she had her growing friendship with Edouard.

'Hi, how are you?' she asked warmly, as he strolled up to her. With a small effort she hid the momentary ache she felt each time she first saw him. It didn't take a genius to figure out how Eugénie Jusserand's brother so frequently knew when Antoine was away from the estate.

'Comme ci, comme ça.' He watched Rémi's sullen, retreating back. 'You certainly bring out the protective instinct in men, Camille. I'd hate to meet Rémi Fouquet in a dark alley.' He grinned suddenly. 'What an injustice to be felled for absolutely no cause, when there are so many men who have genuine reason to avenge their honour.'

'I bet there are legions.'

'Armies. Here I am dancing in attendance, without being offered a silken cheek for a brotherly kiss,' he said sadly, while his eyes twinkled.

'That's because I know what you mean by a brotherly kiss,' she scoffed, clipping a few more green sprouts from a vine. 'Besides, you need a break once in a while from all the hard work it takes to keep up your reputation as a wolf,' she said lightly.

Months ago, Edouard had tried to kiss her the first time he had found her alone. Camille had pulled back.

'I'm married, Edouard,' she had said simply.

Surprisingly—even gratefully, it sometimes seemed to her—he had understood and accepted at once. Since then, a strong, genuinely reciprocated friendship had grown between them. As for Antoine . . . let Antoine assume what he wanted, Camille thought, grimly.

'I had hoped to find you free today,' said Edouard morosely. He stood there, hands in his pockets, watching her work, and looking dejected.

'Actually, I'm just about done,' she said, looking up at him in concern. She had never heard Edouard sound depressed before.

'I need someone to console me during my last meal as a free man,' he said.

'Sounds serious. That must mean you're faced with either marriage or work,' she said, smiling. She took off her gloves and put them in a small wicker workbasket with her clippers.

Edouard took the basket from her as they walked towards the château. 'You laugh, when a fate worse than death looms.'

'Now I know it's work,' she retorted.

'Will you go into Beaune with me and have lunch?'

Camille hesitated. The idea was appealing; she hadn't taken an afternoon off in a long time. 'Let me see how my grandfather is first, all right?'

She left him on the terrace. Madame Gounod was just emerging from Charles Deslandes's room as Camille came down the hall.

'How is he?' Camille asked softly.

Madame Gounod's plump, kindly face was discouraged. 'He's sleeping, but he never touched the fruit drink I made for him.' She shook her head. 'He eats so little now.'

'I know,' said Camille. 'It must be very hard for you to come up with good things to tempt him. I know he appreciates it even if he doesn't have the appetite to eat much.'

The housekeeper's expression lightened a little. 'Will you want lunch soon, *madame*?'

'No, I think I'll go into Beaune for lunch today.'

'A good idea. You have been working too hard, if I may say so. I don't know what Monsieur Antoine is thinking about, letting you do so much.' She frowned at Camille's soiled clothes. 'You work harder than he does '

Camille smiled. 'It's really not his fault. I like working . . . It takes my mind off things.'

'*Tiens*, off you go, and don't worry. I'll keep a close eye on Monsieur Deslandes,' she said kindly.

The restaurant Edouard picked was small, intimate, and discreet. Handing them a menu, the waiter bowed decorously and retreated to call for the champagne Edouard ordered.

'Tell me how crucial your financial situation is before I order,' said Camille, glancing at the expensive menu. 'Or even better, can this be on me?'

'Nonsense. I may have exaggerated the immediacy of my plight to get you away for an afternoon. Order anything you like.' He smiled charmingly at her. 'Actually, my father has merely threatened—rather pointedly, I admit—to find me a job. Business has been in a slump for some time now, and I'm afraid he may be having difficulty supporting Eugénie and me in the style to which we are thoroughly and quite unashamedly accustomed.'

'Do you think he means it?' Camille's mind went back to Joséphine's long-ago hint that Eugénie's interest in Antoine was basically monetary.

Edouard shrugged. 'I must admit he sounded more serious than usual. He does this periodically, you know, and then gives up in despair. What can one do with a person of no skills? No commercially useful skills, I mean, of course,' he added with a smile.

'You're too hard on yourself,' Camille said sternly, 'and I, for one, think you exaggerate your lack of abilities. Actually, you're intelligent, reasonably presentable, and quite charming. In your own way, of course.'

Edouard whistled. 'An ardent supporter! I didn't know I had one.'

'Your problem—'

Edouard rolled his eyes in mock dismay. 'I knew it was too good to be true.'

Camille laughed, then continued '—is that you don't have any focus; you don't have a goal to aim for.'

The waiter returned, rolling a cart on which was a bottle of champagne in a bedewed silver ice bucket. He picked up the bottle, proudly showed the label to Edouard, and wrapped an immaculate white towel around it. Expertly, he gently popped the cork and poured a tiny amount in Edouard's glass.

Edouard tasted it carefully. The waiter hovered anxiously over him. '*Délicieux*,' said Edouard. '*Formidable.*'

Gratified, the waiter filled their glasses, then took their order.

Camille sipped the champagne. It was excellent—bone-dry, with just the right amount of liveliness. 'Edouard,' she said when the waiter left, 'there must be something you really want to do with your life.'

He smiled whimsically, raised an eyebrow, and began to say something flip.

'No,' she interrupted, 'I'm serious.'

Edouard took both her hands lightly between his fingers and looked down at them.

'Are you really interested?'

'Yes!'

His gaze rose to her eyes. He looked intently at her, more serious than she had ever seen him. 'Once upon a time I wanted very badly to become an artist . . . a painter.'

Camille's eyes widened in surprise. 'Why didn't you?'

'My father wouldn't hear of it. I had talent—at least, I think I did—and I wanted desperately to go to art school.' He stopped, apparently embarrassed by his own intensity. He released her hands and took a sip of wine. Staring into his glass, he continued. 'Oh, he hadn't minded paying for lessons when I was a teenager; it was better than some other things I might have done. But he insisted I attend university to study something serious.'

'Why didn't you strike out on your own?'

The first course arrived, a *pâté de foie gras* with fresh crusty bread to spread it on, and they began to eat as they talked.

Edouard bit appreciatively into some *pâté* and

gestured at the champagne. 'Even as a young man I had already acquired a taste for the finer things in life,' he said frankly.

'I forget sometimes,' Camille replied apologetically. 'When people are raised wealthy, it must make it very hard to give up what money can buy.'

Edouard smiled. 'I'm grateful for your tolerance. With a father like yours as an example, I'd expect you to be more severe with a wastrel who chose to be rich rather than be his own man.'

'No, it would be unfair to anyone to hold my father up as a model. I suspect very few people could do what he did.'

'Yet it's exactly what *you* are going to do, isn't it, *ma belle*, when your grandfather dies? Give up Château Villon to Antoine?'

'Château Villon is Antoine's,' she said seriously. 'It was never mine to give up.'

Their main course was served. It was a heavenly concoction of puff pastry surrounding a boned chicken breast, and covered with a satiny sauce of cream, mushrooms, and truffles. Camille tasted the Château Villon Pinot Chardonnay which Edouard had tactfully ordered to go with it. With childlike satisfaction she found the wine was a superb accompaniment to the meal.

'What happened after college?' she asked. 'Did you try to go back to painting?'

Edouard laughed. 'After! I didn't make it through! The university authorities gave me three years, then decided I was spending far too much time in extracurricular activities, and my seat might better be occupied by a serious student.' He shrugged. 'I can't say I blame them. I dabbled in paint a bit after that, but by then, unfortunately, I had become fond of the ladies. And rather addicted to easy living.'

'What's to stop you now?' she asked. 'Don't you think your father would prefer an artist in the family to a . . .' her voice trailed off lamely.

'*Roué?*' Edouard said, lifting an eyebrow in amusement.

'Yes,' she said, grinning.

'He probably would. But he still wouldn't call it work. He's a businessman, you know. Only activities that make money qualify as serious pursuits.'

Thoughtfully, Camille asked, 'Did you do any portraits?'

'A few, why?'

'I was just thinking,' she said, finishing the last luscious bite on her plate. 'Portrait painters can make money if they're good and if they know a lot of people to paint—especially beautiful women.'

'I qualify on the latter if not the former,' Edouard replied.

'Seriously, you could at least try painting again. All you need is a commission to impress your father. Perhaps he'd delay lowering the boom until you're established.'

'Possibly . . . but who would take me seriously enough to give me a commission?'

'I would,' Camille replied calmly. 'You could paint a portrait of me.' Where the idea had come from she hadn't the least idea. But now that she had said it, it sounded rather like fun.

Edouard smiled at her and took a sip of wine. '*Ma belle*, for you I would do anything . . . but certainly not for a fee.' He reached out and lightly brushed back a stray golden curl from her cheek. 'You know, you'd be an intriguing subject to paint—I couldn't ask for any more inspiration to give it a go. But for money, no.'

'Why not? It would have to be a real business arrangement to impress your father, wouldn't it? Besides, I wouldn't feel right about keeping the portrait if I didn't pay for it,' Camille continued with growing enthusiasm. 'I'd show it to François and Hélène Chevillot; I bet Hélène would love to have one of herself. Before you know it, you'll be in demand.'

'Slow down, slow down,' he said, laughing. 'How do you know it will be any good?'

'I just know it will be.' Then she added mischievously, 'You'd become all the rage; all sorts of women will be dying to spend an irreproachable afternoon with so charming a rake as the famous Edouard Jusserand—and have a portrait painted into the bargain.'

An hour later, as Edouard halted the car in the château's driveway, Camille glanced nonchalantly out the window—and was startled at seeing Antoine's tall, lean figure at the threshold. Her heart sank. Before this he had always stayed away the whole day. She reached out and touched Edouard on the arm.

'Don't bother to get out, Edouard,' she said, mustering a light tone. 'I had a lovely meal, and I'll call you tomorrow about arrangements for the portrait.'

Edouard also had seen Antoine. 'Fine, *ma belle*.' His hands were clenched on the steering wheel. 'And . . . call me if you need me for anything else.'

'Of course.' She got out of the car. 'And thanks

again.' As the car pulled away, Camille turned and walked slowly up the steps, taking a deep breath to steady herself.

Antoine stood watching her ascend the stairs, his narrowed icy brown eyes running down her in a scathing glance which made her quail.

'Hello, Antoine,' she said, trying to sound casual as she walked quickly by him, neither expecting nor awaiting a response.

He swivelled, grabbing her arm like a vice, and steered her into the drawing room, closing the door behind him.

'Before this, I only suspected you were amusing yourself with that lecher,' he grated, looking her up and down again, every line of his face insulting her. 'And to think when you were throwing yourself at me in the beginning, I put it down to naïvety. I was *so* careful not to turn you into second-hand goods. What a laugh!'

Shocked by the savagery of his words and tone, Camille threw back her head in a defiant movement, and met his glare head on. Her colour deepened, but her eyes stayed steady. 'Edouard is my friend, nothing more.' She flung the words at him. 'But I don't care what you believe.' Then suddenly she began to sob, and covered her face.

'*Mon dieu,*' he groaned, raising his eyes to the ceiling. 'I can't stand hearing a woman cry. A most unfair tactic.'

But it was as if a dam had broken inside her and all the heartache of the last year was welling up and overflowing. She couldn't have stopped crying if she had wanted to.

Astoundingly, he gathered her into his arms and

gently stroked her hair. 'I'm sorry, Camille, it's just that the thought of you in that snake's arms throws me into a rage.'

Slowly, the forlorn, cold feeling thawed as Camille drew comfort and warmth from the strong pressure of Antoine's embrace.

'He's not a snake,' she sniffled into his shirt, after the tears finally ran dry. She instantly regretted defending Edouard, as she felt Antoine stiffen.

He let his arms fall away from her. 'Let's drop Edouard, shall we?' he said, the hint of warmth in his voice replaced by a chilling arrogance. 'As you re-minded me once, you're not one of my possessions and what you do is your own business.' Antoine turned and moved towards the drinks cabinet. 'Would you like some wine?'

Camille picked up her purse from where she had dropped it and fumbled for a handkerchief.

'No, thank you,' she managed to murmur, feeling as if she were floundering back in the icy seas she had been plucked out of for one brief, exquisite moment when he was holding her. Heartsick she used the one excuse that would automatically allow her to flee from his presence. 'I need to check on *Grand-père*, to make sure he's all right.'

'I just came from his room. He's sleeping.'

Over the months Camille had found Antoine to be as thoughtful and considerate to her grandfather as she was, and out of affection, too, not with thought of future gain. She had learned that much about Antoine Jules de Breze, if little else.

Bereft of an excuse to retreat, Camille sank down on the sofa in front of the fireplace. Henri apparently had started the fire only minutes ago, because the bottom logs were barely ignited. She stared at the wavering orange flames, her hands unconsciously clenched in her lap, while behind her she could hear Antoine pour out the wine. Only when she saw his hand holding the glass out to her did she look up.

'Thank you,' she said softly.

As he sat down beside her, she shifted her gaze back to the fire.

'For the life of me,' he said in a flat voice, 'I don't know what a woman like you sees in Edouard.'

He's just a friend, you stupid, dense idiot, she wanted to scream at him. Can't you see I've never loved anyone but you? But the old fears clutched at her heart, and in any case, he hadn't believed her a few minutes ago when she had tried to explain about Edouard, so she merely shrugged her shoulders and said, 'People are attracted by all sorts of things in others. You're still seeing Eugénie, aren't you? What attracts you to her?' She couldn't resist saying it, and tensed for an explosion that didn't come. It was as if all his fury had drained out with her tears.

Instead he leaned back on the sofa, his shoulder barely touching hers, and stretched out his long legs on the sturdy marble-topped table in front of them. He took a sip of the ruby port and this time it was he who stared into the fire. 'Who knows? Whatever it was, there's less and less of it as time passes.'

She waited for him to go on, but he simply stared moodily into the fire.

'You're doing a fine job on your section,' he said gruffly, after a lengthy and painful silence. 'I fully expected you to have difficulties managing the men and—and making the right decisions. To be honest, I assumed you would fail.'

'I'm sorry to disappoint you.' The moment the words popped out Camille regretted them. 'Forgive me, Antoine, I didn't mean to sound so . . . It was nice of you to compliment me.' She blinked away a new set of tears. '*Grand-père* looks so weak, doesn't he?' she said, turning to the one topic they both could discuss calmly. 'I'm so afraid he won't even make it through the summer.'

'You've got close to him, haven't you?' he said, surprisingly gently, his voice melancholy. 'He's a grand old man and I'll miss him.'

Camille didn't know how long they sat there watching the fire. She just wished she could sit there by his side—unthinking, unreasoning, but drawing warmth from the power of his presence—for ever and ever.

Henri materialised, his face alight with pleasure at finding the two of them sitting so companionably. The conversation in the servants' quarters frequently turned with real regret towards the unfortunate state of affairs between the *monsieur* and *madame*. All found their loyalties painfully torn; all wished only for the marriage to work.

'Monsieur Deslandes is awake and wonders if you might wish to join him for a while,' Henri said deferentially, then handed Camille a letter. 'It came while you were gone, *madame*.'

'Thank you, Henri, we'll go right up.' She examined the return address—the letter was from her father. She moved her fingers over it nervously after Henri left. 'Antoine?'

'Yes?' He had dropped his feet to the floor and straightened up when Henri came into the room.

'I started a sort of campaign, in my letters, to get

my father to come visit *Grand-père*. In the last one, I told him how sick he was. If Dad does agree to come . . .' She paused uncertainly.

'Would I mind?' asked Antoine, his eyebrows raised. 'And would I worry about him trying to claim Château Villon as rightfully his? Is that what you want to know?'

Thankful that he had laid her fears out in the open, she answered, 'Yes, exactly . . . oh, Antoine, Dad wouldn't—'

He raised a finger to her lips to hush her. 'I'm not worried, *ma petite*.' A ghost of a smile flitted across his face. 'Once, long ago, I accused you of something very similar, remember? I know better now.' Her breathing stilled and her heart pounded as his hand touched the back of her neck. 'If Jean Adrien could raise you so free of greed for an inheritance—an inheritance that would have been yours except for unfortunate circumstances—why should I think he would harbour such greed himself?'

Even though their personal relationship was in shreds, and it pained her to have him think she could have an affair while married, she was comforted to hear respect in his voice as he talked about her father. She sighed with relief. 'I'm so glad you feel that way.'

'It's one of the things I admire most in you, Camille. I've wanted to tell you this for a long time, but . . . we haven't been talking much, have we?' His fingers lightly caressed the back of her neck. 'Camille, you move in this environment as if you were born to it, but you've taken no advantage of it . . . you've demanded nothing . . . instead, you've insisted on working. Working very hard and very well.'

So she had gained some of his respect, too. He didn't totally despise her! Camille's heart did a little flip-flop. She looked down, unseeing, at the letter. Antoine gently pushed aside the golden hair that had fallen to obscure her face from him. With his hand at her cheek, he started to say something, then abruptly changed his mind.

'You can open your letter now, *ma petite*,' he said.

She opened the envelope, her slender fingers trembling in excitement. After scanning it quickly, she threw her arms excitedly around him, then jumped up. 'He's coming! Oh, he's coming in just three weeks ... I can't wait to read his letter to *Grand-père*!'

In her excitement, she didn't notice the pain and longing that flickered in Antoine's eyes at her impulsive hug. Slowly, he followed her up the stairs to her grandfather's room.

After breakfast the next morning, Camille found herself alone with her grandfather. Charles Deslandes, sitting up in his bed, pillows plumped behind him, was sipping a second cup of *café au lait*. He had been alternately excited, nervous, and restless since she had broken the news of Jean Adrien's visit, and she had begun to fear his health might be affected. Casting about for a topic that would calm him, she remembered the portrait.

'Did you know Edouard once wanted to be an artist, *Grand-père*?'

Charles Deslandes fixed a steady gaze on his granddaughter.

And what concern is Edouard Jusserand of mine? his eyes said. Or yours? 'Yes, I knew,' he answered brusquely. 'Had some talent, too. I always thought

Jusserand handled that young puppy as badly as I handled your father.' The old man paused, then pushed aside the painful memories. 'Edouard was sent to the university, and all he ever studied was women and the art of intoxication. I must say he learned them very thoroughly.' He swallowed some coffee, and said meditatively, 'Nothing but a sponge now.'

Camille smiled. 'His father thinks so too, and wants him to get a job. Edouard is thinking of taking up painting again.'

Her grandfather snorted.

'I'd like to commission him to paint a small portrait of me,' Camille said.

'Why?'

The question surprised Camille. She hadn't thought about what she would do with it. 'Well, it . . . it would make a nice present for Dad.' She ploughed ahead courageously in the face of his dubious look. 'Edouard doesn't want any money, naturally, but I insisted. After all, he has to prove to his father that there's money to be made. The only problem is that I really don't have any money to speak of.' How ironic that she was asking her grandfather for money the very morning after Antoine had complimented her on her indifference to it.

Charles Deslandes snorted again. 'As if that's my fault. Whenever I try to give you some, you tell me you don't need it.' He paused, and then said, 'A portrait, eh?'

'Yes, *Grand-père*.' Camille held her breath.

'Not a bad idea, actually,' he said with a gleam in his eye.

Camille expelled her breath in relief.

'But he needs to do something more than a small one if he wants to catch the public's attention. Now a full-length picture with you in that green gown—and the Deslandes emeralds as well—might be quite impressive.'

Camille started to protest. 'Oh, no, that would be too—'

He cut her off. 'It would make a handsome first anniversary present for me to give Antoine.'

The proposal startled her. 'I'm not sure Antoine would like something like that—'

He gestured impatiently. 'Do you think I'm unaware that things still aren't working out between you two stubborn fools?'

'Oh, *Grand-père*,' she said, 'you're wrong—'

'Pah! One could take all the brains between you and they would fit on the head of a pin.'

She shook her head in exasperation at him.

'You two simpletons are in love and both of you are too proud to admit it.' He was right about *her*, Camille thought leadenly; too bad he wasn't right about Antoine. He shook his head back at her. 'It will come out right,' he said firmly, 'but at the rate you're going, I won't live to see it.'

She reached out and took his hand. It was so worn and thin her heart constricted. 'Please don't say that, *Grand-père*. Of course it will come out right, and of course you'll be here to see it.' To change the painful subject and calm him—she was distressed by his grey pallor—she said, 'A full-sized portrait would certainly give Edouard a chance to show what he could do. And maybe Antoine *would* like it.' She leaned over, kissed him, and gently hugged his frail shoulders.

'*Bon*,' he said. 'I'll have my lawyer make the financial arrangements. Perhaps the Chevillots will let him use one of their rooms. That way we can keep it a surprise for Antoine.' The colour was already returning to his face, but as a kind of afterthought he frowned grumpily. 'I insist on a chaperone, you understand.'

Camille laughed. 'I'll ask Hélène to be our chaperone, but really *Grand-père*, you don't have to worry. Edouard and I are just good friends.'

He grunted. 'Any man in his right mind would worry about leaving a beautiful woman alone too long with Edouard Jusserand.'

CHAPTER EIGHT

CAMILLE looked up from her work to find Antoine idly leaning one arm against a trellis stake and watching her. Ever since the night a week before, when they had sat quietly watching the fire, the barrier between them had begun to crumble, and he had taken to dropping by her section of the vineyard. He rarely said much, although sometimes it seemed as if he were on the verge of speaking. Usually he just glowered at her a while and left. Although these taciturn visits were painful for Camille, there was also an exquisite but restrained happiness at simply being in his presence . . . and at knowing something was drawing him to her.

'I see you're taking after Rémi,' she said lightly, her heart accelerating. Today, she would challenge him to converse.

'In what way?'

'He comes around, too, to watch me prune,' she said with a faint smile, 'and to worry. He's afraid I'm cutting back too much.'

Antoine shrugged his broad, powerful shoulders. 'He's mumbled something like that to me.'

'And are you worried?' she asked, moving to inspect the progress of another vine.

'Not much. Just watching your assurance inspires confidence,' he answered casually. Then to her surprise he picked up the conversational ball. 'How did you learn so much so young?'

Camille shrugged. 'I guess it was because I started so early. When my mother died, our vineyard was barely beginning to turn a profit. There was enough money to live on, but not enough to hire someone to take care of me. Dad and Bernie had no choice but to let me tag along while they worked.'

'It still doesn't explain how you picked up so much,' Antoine said seriously. 'I could watch Rémi all day and still not be able to do some of the tasks—like pruning. It's more art than skill, I think.'

'You're just like my father.' Camille stopped working, and she too leaned an arm against a stake. 'Dad followed Bernie around as a child, too, and watched just the way I did, but from a different perspective.' She grinned at Antoine. 'The perspective of someone who was going to be the owner some day,' she said, absent-mindedly twisting a grape leaf between her fingers.

'I see . . . and you saw yourself actually doing the work?'

'I think so. I think I sensed pretty early that Dad was good at the business end, but in the vineyard I was more help to Bernie than he was.'

She looked up at him, slightly embarrassed at how egotistical it all sounded. 'Not that Dad wasn't very good . . .'

'But you were even better?'

'Bernie seemed to think so. He took a great deal of time to tutor me.' She grinned. 'I think he saw me as another vine—unruly but with possibilities—that had sprung up in his vineyard and needed pruning.'

Antoine actually laughed. 'He certainly produced quite a flower.'

She pretended to ignore his comment, but her

heart beat crazily. 'Whenever I did something wrong—some childish prank—it was Bernie who disciplined me.'

'Because you could wrap Jean Adrien around your little finger without half trying?' he teased.

Her blush gave her away. 'It'll be good to see my father. I'm sorry they both can't leave the vineyard at the same time, and Bernie has to wait until after the harvest to visit.'

Camille glanced down at her wristwatch. 'It's already ten! I'd better hurry; I told Pierre to have the car ready for me in just half an hour.' At his frown, she added hesitantly, 'I need to do some more shopping.'

'Again?' A storm cloud passed over Antoine's features. In one second her words had wiped out the tenuous thread of communication that had been developing for a week. 'Didn't you spend all Tuesday morning shopping?'

'Unfortunately, I didn't find anything I liked. I promise not too spend too much,' she said, trying desperately to sound gay as she deliberately misinterpreted his words. What a stupid excuse she picked, she thought miserably. Antoine knew she wasn't the sort of female to go shopping twice in one week.

His face hardened into a mask of steel and his dark eyes revealed a chilling, ominous anger. 'So now you need to slink off to your lover twice in one week? Is this what you mean by being discreet?'

The words plunged like daggers into Camille's heart. With her colour high, she turned away before he could see the tears that welled up in her eyes and blinded her. Blinking them back, she walked towards the château, feeling his piercing eyes boring holes in her back. It took all her inborn sense of dignity to walk in carefully controlled steps, her shoulders straight, her head high, when all she wanted to do was to run and throw herself off the nearest cliff—except that she would never give him the satisfaction.

Maybe she should have told him about the portrait sittings, she thought, trying to pull together her shattered emotions. Her wounded sense of pride deepened. No, she wouldn't give that unbending, infuriating man the time of day, much less tell him about the portrait. Besides, she had promised her grandfather she'd keep it a surprise. Some surprise! Antoine would probably burn it as soon as *Grand-père* was gone.

With that grim thought, she quickly bathed and changed into a pale blue afternoon frock. Then she carefully packed her emerald-green gown and necklace into a shoulder bag.

Pierre was waiting for her, and within minutes he had deposited her at the Chevillots' château and retreated to the garage to argue about cars with their chauffeur. Waving to her from the terrace was Hélène, looking beautiful in a red, brightly patterned sundress.

'It's awfully nice of you and François to let us impose on you in this way,' said Camille as she joined her, 'and to put up Edouard for the duration.' Her voice was carefree and friendly; she wasn't going to advertise her troubles to the world.

'It's no imposition at all,' assured Hélène. Then she added, slightly pouting, 'Although I did expect, as chaperone, to have to fend off Edouard's advances to the two of us. But I think you've created a monster, Camille.'

'What do you mean?' she asked anxiously.

'He worked all day on Tuesday after you left, and then yesterday, and this morning he was up painting before breakfast.

'Really!' cried Camille, genuinely delighted at the thought. Maybe something good would yet come out of this mess. It wasn't much comfort, but she could use all the comfort she could get.

'The only thing I've heard from him this morning was a grumble about the inconvenience of not having his model always on call.'

Camille laughed. 'Then I'd better change right away.'

Ten minutes later the emerald-gowned, emerald-bedecked Madame de Breze joined Edouard in the little study set aside for his use. He had put his easel before a window with strong northern light, and had commandeered an old table for his supplies.

'*Bon*,' he said, looking up with a preoccupied expression when she entered. 'Just in time. I finished as much of the table and background as I can do today. Now stand just the way you did on Tuesday.'

Camille moved to a graceful Louis XVI table in the middle of the room and took up the pose, turning her shoulders slightly away from him, but her face directly towards him, with one hand casually placed on the edge of the table.

The change in Edouard was amazing. He was dressed casually in a paint-spattered blue work-shirt and jeans. She noted with amusement, however, that the jeans had a designer label. It wasn't just his clothing, though. Gone was the languid, jaded man about town. In its place was the boyish and vulnerable person that she had only once or twice before seen peeping out. More important, he looked intent and thoroughly competent.

She eyed with interest the rich, muted tones he was mixing on his palette, and asked, 'Can't I see what you've done so far?'

'Absolutely not; not until it's finished.' He looked up, set down his palette knife, and walked up to her.

'Almost right, but not quite.' He turned her shoulders a little more, and tilted her chin a bit. His hands were impersonal, as if he were arranging a bowl of lemons for a still-life.

'Parfait.' He went back to the canvas and immediately set to work.

Camille enjoyed seeing him so absorbed. If not for Antoine, she thought—trying in vain to remember what it had been like before she had fallen so helplessly and hopelessly in love with him—she might have fallen for Edouard. From the beginning she had sensed that his *bon vivant* role had been assumed in reaction to some old sadness or loss.

The minutes began to drag, though, as she found her muscles rebelling against holding the same position for so long. And her smile was starting to feel pasted on.

'Edouard, may I have a break?' she asked when she could stand it no longer.

'Don't move yet,' he said sharply.

'Hélène was right, I've created a monster,' she wailed.

Ignoring her, he painted on silently for another few minutes. *'Bon,'* he muttered softly, placing his paint brush between his teeth, and looking at the canvas. Abruptly he remembered Camille and looked apologetic.

'*Oui* . . . a break, *naturellement*.' Smiling contritely, he added, 'Sorry about posing you for so long. I guess I was somewhat engrossed.'

'Engrossed!' she exclaimed, stretching with relief. 'Try obsessed!' She laughed. 'I think it's tremendous.'

Hearing conversation, Hélène poked her head in the doorway and said impishly, 'Do the maestro and his model have a few moments for coffee out on the terrace?'

Shaking his head, Edouard laughed. 'Women!' he said, throwing his hands up and feigning a tragic expression. 'Always admonishing a man to do something useful, and then when he does, they tempt him with play.'

Grinning, he cleaned his hands with a cloth soaked in turpentine. 'I'll join you soon as I've washed up.'

The break passed quickly, with chatting about painting, drinking coffee, and munching the delicious strawberry tartlets the cook had baked for them.

'Ready for another go at it?' Edouard asked as soon as he had finished his coffee.

'A slave-driver is what I've turned him into, Hélène,' Camille said mournfully, quickly finishing her own cup. 'I think I'd have preferred a monster.'

Hélène, not the slightest bit fooled, heard the pride in Camille's voice, and so did Edouard.

The days dragged by and every morning Camille woke with a leaden heaviness. Tuesdays and Thursdays, the days of the portrait sittings, were the worst. Antoine's temper was brittle and he was easily aroused. Camille knew that as estate manager—and even worse in Antoine's eyes, as Camille's suppor-ter—Rémi Fouquet was bearing the brunt of his anger. Although it was impossible for Camille to share her troubles with Rémi, she did attempt to keep him from quitting, something which he had hinted at.

'It will pass, Rémi. You know it's me he's angry with.'

'You're telling me. Yesterday I simply mentioned your section and he almost bit my head off,' said Rémi grimly, his weatherbeaten face clouded.

Camille smiled wanly. 'I'm sorry, Rémi. I don't think things will go on like this much longer.' No, she thought bleakly as she left to visit her grandfather, not with Charles Deslandes fading the way he was. When he no longer needed her, she would leave at the first possible minute.

She was spending as much time as possible with her grandfather. Charles Deslandes had become increasingly nervous about seeing Jean Adrien. He feared the visit—after so many years—would turn out to be a disaster. He wasn't the only one. Camille feared Antoine wasn't even going to be civil to her father when he came. She knew it was only her youthful health and irrepressible vitality that kept her from cracking under the strain.

'Don't worry so much, *Grand-père*,' said Camille, trying to reassure him one afternoon when he was particularly fretful. 'He wouldn't come all this way just to have a fight.'

*

'Camille, stop wiggling!' exclaimed Edouard with a frown. It was the sixth sitting and possibly the last.

'I'm not wiggling . . . I'm just moving my foot a little. It's asleep.'

Edouard looked up and smiled. 'If you can hold your head still for just five minutes longer, I think we can call it a day. In fact, I think it's about finished altogether.'

'Really? Will you finally let me see it?' she asked shyly.

Both Camille and Helene had been in torturous suspense about the portrait's progress. Between them, they had manufactured all sorts of ingenious reasons as to why he should let them examine it, but he hadn't allowed them even a peek.

The minutes dragged by, seeming more like fifty than five. Finally Edouard, sighing, set down his palette and brushes. 'It's done,' he said flatly, his tone suddenly guarded. 'Come, tell me what you think.'

Although Camille had seen herself gowned and jewelled many times in the past year, it was no preparation for what she saw now. The Camille who looked back at her was not only extraordinarily beautiful, she was mature and confident. And she was at ease in the world of wealth and polite society that Edouard had somehow suggested in muted tones of oil on canvas. Partly, it was the skill with which he had captured the silk and chiffon of her gown, her skin tones, the deep, mysterious glow of the emeralds. But there was something more, something indefinable. Edouard had seen in her—and put on canvas—the Camille that she longed to be.

Wide-eyed, she gazed so long, so silently, that

Edouard impatiently moved his hand up and down in front of her eyes.

'Shocked because it's so good or so bad?' he asked in a forced light tone.

'It's magnificent of course,' she said softly, 'but Edouard . . .' She laughed uncertainly. 'She—'

'Ah,' said Edouard, 'so far so good. "She", not "it".'

'She looks like . . . like the reigning queen of Paris society.' She turned to him in confusion. 'It's me and yet it isn't me.'

Now it was Edouard's turn to laugh. 'I've painted the woman you'll become.' He grinned at her. 'Not the child you still are.'

'Child!' She stamped on the floor, then bit her lip. Stamping was a child's gesture. So was biting one's lip. Nevertheless, she was angry with him. 'How can you call me a child?'

'You *are* a child, and you will be until a man has . . . until you've been loved by a man in the way a man loves.' His voice turned husky, and he traced the line of her cheek with his hand. 'That stupid, blind Antoine! How I wish that I . . .' Abruptly, he turned to his work table and began to clean up and organise. 'One of these days I'm going to pound some sense into his thick skull.'

Camille sighed. 'Perhaps, if I'm lucky, I'll get over him,' she said. 'But the painting, Edouard—over-sophisticated or not, it's fantastic . . . beautiful.'

She stared intently at it, then shook her head. 'It's shocking to think your father discouraged you.'

'Not really. I assure you I never painted this well before. I knew techniques—how to paint cloth, flesh, all the rest—but my figures were wooden, lifeless; no

depth.' His eyes suddenly twinkled. 'Perhaps my . . .
adventures have taught me to see more in a woman
than mere surfaces.'

Camille giggled, 'I can see it now as an art school
course: The Art of Don Juanism and its Function in
Portrait Painting, three units, taught by the experienced Professor Edouard Jusserand.'

He laughed. 'That's one course I'd love to teach,
especially if there's any laboratory work. Seriously,
do you think your grandfather will like it?'

'He'll love it,' she said eagerly. 'Can we show it to
him right now? I could call Henri and see if the coast
is clear. If I remember, Antoine said something
about going to Chagny today.' To the butler of
course. Antoine hadn't exchanged two consecutive
words with her since that morning in the vineyard,
except in front of her grandfather. But that didn't
count; she and Antoine, fearful of hurting him, were
getting good at acting in his presence.

'*Certainement*, I don't see why not. But we'll have to
be careful. Some of the face is still wet. Camille,' he
said with growing excitement, 'do you suppose he'd
let me enter it in an art competition in Paris next
week? I'd have it back well before your anniversary.'

'What an exciting thought!' she cried. 'Just think
of the publicity if it got accepted!'

Camille called Henri while Edouard showed
Hélène the portrait. From the cries of delight, Camille knew that Edouard would be getting a second
commission.

Charles Deslandes was sitting in his study, impatiently waiting for them. Edouard fussily placed the
portrait where the light was best for viewing, then

stepped back self-consciously. Camille stood near her grandfather, trying unsuccessfully to read his expression. He gazed at it even longer than she had, and she grew increasingly nervous. Edouard's quick glances at her, she noticed, were also more than a little jittery.

'You know quite well what I think of it,' the old man said suddenly.

'I know I made her a bit more mature—' Edouard began, trying to hide his disappointment.

'Don't be a fool!' the old man said, cutting him off. 'It's a masterpiece and you could have said so yourself when you set it down.'

Camille and Edouard grinned at each other in delight. They both started talking at once, stopped, started again, and laughed. At last, between the two of them, they got Monsieur Deslandes's permission to let Edouard exhibit the painting.

'I don't see why not,' he said, patting Camille's hand, 'as long as it's back by your anniversary.'

The next day was the long-awaited date of Jean Adrien's arrival. Pierre was to drive Camille to the railway station in Dijon to meet him. Antoine was nowhere to be seen when Camille left. She just prayed he'd continue to play his share of the charade and not decide in his unpredictable, high-handed way, to reveal to her father the real state of their relationship.

The platform was thronged with disembarking passengers when she arrived, and she anxiously combed the crowd for her father's familiar figure.

'Camille!' She heard her name called from behind her. As she turned two strong arms enveloped her, and she found herself crying tears of joy against his jacket. Jean Adrien beamed down at her as she pulled away.

'You look great, Dad!'

He did, too. Gone were the worry and fatigue she had seen in his face the day she left. The faint touches of grey at his temples and sideburns were new, but they made him look more distinguished. And he was wearing a flawlessly cut new suit.

'There aren't any words to describe how you look, honey,' he said, grinning. 'Whatever happened to my little tomboy?'

Camille glanced down at the classic lines of her expensive print dress, and the co-ordinated bag and shoes. 'Isn't it incredible what money can do?' she responded impishly.

'Uh-uh,' drawled Jean Adrien. 'Only if there's good material to work with in the first place.'

Camille blushed with pleasure, but a sudden thought hit her and she said, 'Dad, you needn't worry that I'm spoiled. I'm still me. And I have enough clothes to last for ever when I get home.'

Jean Adrien picked up his suitcase with one hand and, dropping the other affectionately on his daughter's shoulder, led the way to the exit. 'Oh, I think we can afford to buy you a few new clothes occasionally, especially now.'

'Now?'

'I didn't tell you in a letter because I wanted to surprise you.'

'What?' she asked excitedly.

'Just a few weeks after I wrote to you about IMBEC wanting to buy our grapes, they offered Bernie and me some part-time consulting contracts—extremely well-paid contracts—and we've been working with them on and off all year. Figured we might as well join them if we couldn't beat them.'

'That's wonderful. Do you think grandfather . . .' She broke off in confusion.

'Naturally, he must have dropped a suggestion in someone's ear,' he said tranquilly, 'but they have a smart management team and a good operation. They'd never offer us anything without deciding we were good. Anyway, Bernie's in charge of developing an improved Pinot Noir—with our grapes, of course. And I'm giving them help in distribution and vineyard management.'

'Sounds great,' she exclaimed, 'but I hope you two aren't working too hard.'

Jean Adrien laughed. 'No, just the opposite. We've hired two new men and a housekeeper.'

She smiled with pleasure. 'Oh, Dad, I'm so glad, and it's so nice to see you. Thank you for coming.' She reached for his hand on her shoulder and squeezed it.

'For that you can thank Bernie. I found out he's almost as big a rogue as my father.'

Camille didn't have time to ask for an explanation because Pierre caught sight of them.

'Monsieur Deslandes!'

Camille was momentarily confused, but of course Pierre was addressing her father.

The two men shook hands and clapped each other excitedly on the back. Pierre's delight was so transparent that Camille liked him all the more.

On the drive home, Camille watched her father drink in the sights of his native land hungrily.

'You've missed France, haven't you?' she asked, squeezing his hand again.

'Only sometimes, *ma chérie*, only sometimes.' He shrugged his shoulders. 'I've wanted to visit, all right, but I wouldn't want to return for good. Now tell me about you. I see something very grave in those pretty green eyes that wasn't there before. This "arrangement" with your husband—it isn't working out?'

'I'm fine, really.' Even to her father Camille couldn't reveal her misery. 'Worried about Grandfather of course. He's a dear.'

Jean Adrien laughed. 'He's an old devil, but we Deslandes have always known how to charm the ladies.'

'You won't say anything to hurt him, will you, Dad?' She asked pleadingly, anxiety in her eyes. 'He's truly sorry for the past, and he's so frail now.'

'Don't worry,' he said, leaning over to give her a quick hug. 'What happened wasn't all his fault; I know that. I had a hand in it, too. I'll be on my best behaviour, I promise.'

Camille smiled with relief.

'Tell me about this so-called husband of yours. I only remember him as a skinny kid of ten.'

She suddenly looked out the window. 'Handsome, industrious, kind . . .'

'That sounds like a rehearsed speech if I've ever heard one. Now,' he said gently but firmly, 'tell me what you really think about him.'

'He's an overbearing, dense blockhead,' she said, her eyes brilliant with tears, 'and I can't wait until I see the last of him.' She turned her face to the window and stared unseeingly through it.

'It sounds to me as if somebody is in love with someone,' said Jean Adrien.

Camille shrugged and then, controlling her emotions, she turned and smiled briefly. 'Whatever it sounds like, it's been ghastly, and I can't wait to come home.'

Jean Adrien sighed. 'I know one thing, *ma petite*. I won't renew old quarrels with my father, that I promise—but if Antoine de Breze ever hurts my little girl, I'll wring his neck,' he said, with a flash of genuine menace in his voice.

'You'll do no such thing, Father!' she said fiercely. 'I've been dumped in his lap and . . . and everything . . .' Her voice trailed off. She couldn't bear to think of the two of them fighting.

Jean Adrien threw back his head and laughed, 'You're right. And I'll bet you've been a handful, too! I should know. Beautiful, it's true, but very definitely a handful.'

'Dad!' she exclaimed, poking him in the ribs. 'Wait a minute, I thought you were on my side.'

'Ah, but you just reminded me we men should stick together.'

'You're terrible! All of you!' she said, but she couldn't help smiling as he dropped an affectionate kiss on her forehead.

To Camille's relief, Antoine met them graciously at the door, the façade intact. If he had any qualms about what Jean Adrien's return might mean to him, he didn't show it. He extended his hand with forthright friendliness.

'I'm glad to meet you, Monsieur Deslandes, after all these years,' he said, sounding as if he meant it.

'Jean Adrien, *s'il vous plaît*.'

Nervously, Camille watched them size each other

up as they shook hands, but relaxed as they exchanged pleasantries and old memories.

Henri and Madame Gounod were standing formally in the hall, waiting to greet Jean Adrien. Henri had tears in his eyes and Madame Gounod was crying freely. They both had been in service at Château Villon when he was born, they had been there when he'd left, and they were overjoyed at being there for the reunion they had never expected to come about.

Antoine stood back and let the three of them chatter, laugh, and weep for a while before he finally broke in. 'I'm sure you'll want to go up to your father. He's been extremely anxious.'

Camille walked up the broad staircase with Jean Adrien, who caressed the dark, polished banister as if it were a loved thing. When they approached Charles Deslandes's door, he turned and laid a hand gently on her arm.

'I'd like to see him alone first, *ma petite*. Then I'll have him call you.'

'Of course, Dad, I understand.'

Leaving him, Camille walked to her sitting room. At first she tried to read, but couldn't concentrate, so she paced the room, barely resisting the impulse to bite her nails. At least there wasn't any shouting from down the corridor, she thought thankfully, as the time dragged on.

It was a full hour later when Henri knocked on her door.

'Monsieur Deslandes wishes to see you, *madame*,' he said, his old eyes still sparkling with excitement. 'It's so good to see Monsieur Jean Adrien after all these years.'

With trembling fingers, Camille turned the handle on the door and entered her grandfather's rooms. She walked through the empty study and found them in his bedroom.

Charles Deslandes was sitting up in his bed, with pillows propped up behind him, and Jean Adrien had drawn a chair to his side. Camille's throat caught at the sight of her father's strong, tanned hand lying over her grandfather's pale, thin one.

With the other hand, the old man beckoned her to perch on the side of the bed.

'Camille, I need some intelligent support,' he said. 'Can you believe this young upstart has actually been trying to tell me that the Americans can make wine as well as the French?'

Camille wanted everything to be a pleasure for her grandfather that evening, and when she changed for dinner she took special care with her toilette. Apparently she was successful; Charles Deslandes and Jean Adrien both greeted her with appreciative glances as she entered the drawing room in a new gown, a romantic, old-fashioned creation of thin muslin, with yards and yards of ruffled material in the skirt, and lace on the demure, high-necked bodice. Antoine's convivial mask slipped for a second and he scowled at her fiercely, but he recovered his composure before the other two men noticed.

'An aperitif, Camille?' Antoine asked, his voice studiedly neutral. He went to the crystal decanter on the other side of the room.

'Yes, please.'

He poured her drink, but stood there, forcing her to join him.

'You look stunningly beautiful tonight,' he said, for her ears alone. His mouth curled contemptuously. She could see controlled anger in the clean, masculine planes of his face. 'A vision of virginal purity, one might say. If one didn't know better.'

Camille glanced down at the liquid in the glass he had given her. She toyed momentarily with throwing it in his face. But the effect wouldn't be like water dousing a flame; it would be the flicker that blew up the volcano, and she was determined that tonight would be as perfect as she could make it.

Her green, gold-flecked eyes steadily looked back at him. Then, wordlessly, she left him. Fortunately, her father and grandfather were deep in conversation and hadn't seen the exchange. As she joined them she was aware of Antoine's burning eyes watching her every movement.

Charles Deslandes had insisted on joining them for dinner. Although he ate and drank little of the delicious meal Antoine had asked the cook to prepare, his obvious pleasure as he sat at the head of the table with his family, lightened everyone's heart.

Antoine was a flawless host. The vintage wines he instructed Henri to bring up from the cellar for each course got more and more rare as the evening progressed, and he and Jean Adrien relaxed in each other's company. Indeed, they appeared to be developing a real rapport.

After dinner, with a great deal of good-natured grumbling, Charles Deslandes retired, grandly announcing they hadn't drunk so many great wines at one sitting since 1944, when the German retreat was announced. The rest of them adjourned to the drawing room to sip some early nineteenth-century Napoleon brandy that Henri must have dug up in the farthest reaches of the cellar.

Savouring the cognac, Camille listened to Antoine and her father argue amiably—about wine, naturally: the merits of Napa Valley wine versus that of the Côte-d'Or. She was just letting her mind float blankly, thinking about nothing . . . or anything.

Lost in her thoughts, she was startled to see her father's face looming above her. 'We thought you'd gone to sleep,' he murmured, then teased, 'You've had far too much wine for someone your age.'

She smiled mistily at him. 'It isn't having any effect on me,' she retorted lightly. She realised as she said it that her head was deliciously light. 'Well, maybe a tiny bit,' she confessed with a giggle.

'I hope you won't pay for it tomorrow. Well, you've given me a splendid welcome, Antoine,' he said. 'What an evening. Well, I think I'll leave you two and call it a night.' He kissed Camille's cheek, clapped Antoine on the shoulder, and left.

As soon as Jean Adrien was gone, Antoine's face hardened, and the lava of the volcano rose to the surface. His powerful hands grasped her shoulders.

She stared wide-eyed up at him, paralysed by the suddenness of his attack.

'I swore I'd never touch you again, but maybe I was wrong.' He ground the words out through clenched teeth, in a terrifying rage. 'Maybe if I'd taken you after all, I wouldn't care if you had fifty lovers.'

He bent to find her mouth before she could move. She struggled, but the fierceness of his kiss and his strength overwhelmed her, and he bruisingly forced her mouth to open. At last he lifted his head and she pressed a shaking hand to her burning lips.

His eyes glittered furiously, hypnotically. 'I won't take any more. I'm warning you and you can pass it on to your lover before I break his neck . . . or yours.'

The door of the drawing room had slammed shut before she was able to break out of her trance.

CHAPTER NINE

'YOUR *café au lait, madame.*'

At first the voice barely penetrated Camille's consciousness, and she mentally repeated the meaningless syllables slowly to herself. Her head aching and her throat parched, she finally opened her eyes to find Joséphine, breakfast tray in hand, looking down at her. The expression on her face, bleak and sober, told Camille something terrible had happened.

'*Grand-père?*' she asked, suddenly wide awake.

'*Oui, madame*, the doctor is with him now—'

Camille flung aside the covers without waiting for her to finish, and seized a robe.

Her father and Antoine, standing together near the fireplace, looked up in unison as she entered the study. The bedroom door was ominously closed.

'He isn't . . . ?' she asked desperately, like a frightened child.

Jean Adrien opened his arms and she flew into them. 'Calm down, *ma petite*,' he said, holding her tight. 'No, he isn't. But it doesn't look good. Henri wasn't able to wake him this morning, and so we called the doctor.'

Camille burst into tears. 'I should never have let him come down last night,' she sobbed, her voice muffled against his shoulder.

'It's not your fault,' he said sadly. 'If anything, it was my visit.'

166

Antoine turned his dark head swiftly towards the two of them. He placed his hand firmly on Jean Adrien's shoulder. 'It's nobody's fault ... It's a miracle he lived this long.'

Antoine then moved his hand to briefly touch Camille's head. 'Every man would like an evening like that to be his last,' he said softly. 'I never saw him so happy.'

The door to the bedroom opened. They turned silently to face the doctor as he emerged.

'I'm sorry, but he's gone,' he said gravely. 'I'm sure you've been expecting it for some time.' He looked sympathetically at Jean Adrien. 'Don't feel it was your visit, Monsieur Deslandes,' he said, as if he had heard their conversation, 'I think that's all that kept him alive these last few weeks.'

'Thank you, doctor,' murmured Jean Adrien gratefully.

'May we go in now?' asked Antoine, his voice husky.

The doctor nodded his head.

Camille, tears streaming down her cheeks, turned at once and fled to her room to collapse grief-stricken on her bed. The thought that that beloved old face would never smile at her again, or frown in its gentle way, was more than she could bear. Never again to play chess with him, never to feel the touch of that dry, loving hand ...

In the study, Antoine began to follow her, but Jean Adrien laid a restraining hand on his arm.

'Let her go,' he said, his voice ineffably sad. 'She'll need to cry it out. She was too young for her mother's death to touch her much, you know, so this is really her first loss; always—' shadows of painful memories flashed in his eyes and his voice was far away '—always the hardest.'

In the next terrible days Camille was so shocked and bereft nothing mattered. She was no help at all with the arrangements and with the flood of guests—family and old friends—who descended on Château Villon for the funeral. Only hard work in the vineyard or lonely, rambling evening walks on the hills above the estate, did anything to ease her grief. Out of respect, she joined the others for the funeral and the meal afterwards, but the rest of the time she avoided people, especially Antoine, taking meals in her room.

'She'll kill herself with overwork,' said Rémi one morning to Jean Adrien. 'It's been a week now, and she works from dawn to dusk. And Joséphine says she hardly eats anything.'

'I'll talk to her,' Jean Adrien responded reassuringly. 'I was just thinking it was about time.'

Camille was thinning out the branch tips of some vines when her father found her. She glanced at him.

'Hi, Dad,' she said briefly, then returned to her work.

Jean Adrien's heart wrenched as he took in the new fragility about her features.

'Come on, Camille,' he said gently. 'It's time to let go of the pain a little. You have to start coming out of it.'

Silent, face averted, she continued working.

'You have Antoine worried, and Rémi, and even the servants—and they have enough on their minds coping with their own feelings, let alone all the arrangements that had to be made. And what about getting ready for the harvest next month?' He deliberately made his voice stern.

'I'm sorry, Dad,' she said, still not looking at him. But she had stopped working and was staring at the ground. 'It's been selfish of me to not even help out. It's just that it's . . . it's . . .'

'I know, *ma jeune fille.*' He put his arm around her. 'It hurts. But your grandfather wouldn't have wanted you to be like this.'

'I know.' She toyed nervously with the clippers in her hands, then looked up at him and smiled, her eyes bright with tears. 'All right. I'll finish this row and then come in for lunch, okay?'

Showered and changed into a simple dark brown frock, Camille steeled herself to meet a sea of stares as she entered the dining room a little late. It was disconcerting to find only one person there besides Antoine and her father. In her preoccupation, she hadn't realised all the other guests had left.

The three men leaped to their feet when she entered. Antoine pulled out a chair for her, his dark eyes enigmatic and brooding.

'Camille, this is Monsieur Motte, your grandfather's solicitor,' said her father, introducing her to the austere-looking, grey-haired man. Jean Adrien's face showed both pride and relief at her appearance.

'*Bonjour*, Madame de Breze,' said Monsieur Motte.

'*Bonjour*, Monsieur Motte. I'm sorry I kept you all waiting.' Her voice sounded remote in her ears. Inside, her stomach had knotted. Her grandfather's solicitor! All the thoughts and worries about the future that she had pushed aside rushed into her mind.

Henri entered with the first course. He beamed when he saw Camille, much as Joséphine had when she heard Camille would be going down for lunch. She nodded to Henri, mustering a smile, guilty at the thought that she really had worried everyone.

The food tasted like sawdust but she forced herself to eat most of it and to occasionally join the conversation.

'Shall we adjourn to the drawing room?'

Camille heard Antoine's words with relief. 'Shall I leave you now?' she asked hesitantly.

Monsieur Motte half bowed in her direction. 'If you don't mind, please stay, *madame*. Your presence is required for the reading of the will, and I should like to return to Paris this afternoon.'

In the drawing room she took the seat Jean Adrien indicated, and sat tensely. She prayed her grandfather had kept his promise, because all she wanted now was to have no legal complications to detain her in France.

She couldn't help glancing at Antoine to see if she could tell what he was thinking. But no, his face was smooth as a mask as he closed the huge double doors behind them.

'Now,' said Monsieur Motte, opening the locked briefcase he had set earlier on a side table. He pulled out a sheaf of papers. 'Two months ago Monsieur Deslandes drew up a new will.'

Camille's heart stopped. Oh no, he couldn't have! He couldn't possibly have changed his will after giving her his promise! She shot a glance at Antoine and saw a shadow flit across his solemn, handsome face. What did he fear? The loss of Château Villon, or being shackled for life to her, she wondered.

'It's a very straightforward document,' said Monsieur Motte, putting on wire-rimmed spectacles, then looking at the will. 'There are some preliminary small bequests to servants and a few distant relatives. You can read them at your leisure.' He glanced up at them over his spectacles. 'If that meets with your approval?'

'Of course,' said Antoine in a steady voice.

Jean Adrien was sitting in a chair looking calm and unconcerned.

Monsieur Motte took off his glasses, polished them with a handkerchief, put them back on, and dropped his eyes down to the document. 'To my son Jean Adrien, and my beloved granddaughter Camille, I leave all my stock in the IMBEC Corporation to share and share alike.'

Looking up, he glanced at the two of them and said, 'I might add his holdings were substantial, and will provide you with a very nice income, plus a major voice in company decisions.' Not giving them a chance to respond, he turned back to the document and continued reading.

'I devise and bequeath all the residue of my real and personal property, including Château Villon, to my grand-nephew Antoine Jules de Breze, to be his absolutely, in testimony of my gratitude for his many years of affection and assistance.' Monsieur Motte stopped, took off his glasses, and put them in a metal case.

As Camille realised the solicitor had finished, relief surged through her. He had kept his promise! While Monsieur Motte shuffled the papers together and put them in the briefcase, Jean Adrien moved to Antoine's side and soberly shook his hand.

'My father told me when I came that he was leaving Château Villon to you,' Jean Adrien said frankly, 'and I want to tell you what I told him—that in all honesty, it was the only fair thing to do.'

Monsieur Motte walked to the door. With his hand resting on the door handle, he turned towards them and said to Antoine, 'There is a great deal of paperwork to be examined and signed, Monsieur de Breze, and I'm afraid you will have to come to Paris for a few days to look into it.'

'Fine,' said Antoine, 'I'll come at the end of next week.'

'I'm sorry,' said Monsieur Motte, 'but time is of the essence. Can you come early tomorrow morning?' When Antoine hesitated, he added, 'I would not ask if it were not extremely important for Château Villon.'

Antoine sighed. 'I'll be there at nine o'clock.'

Camille excused herself and left at once. When she reached her room she went out on to the terrace and gazed down on the valley. The green mosaic of the vineyards gracing the long, low hills was breathtakingly beautiful, as it always was. She would miss Château Villon, and she doubted if she would ever stop loving Antoine, in spite of herself. But she was glad it was over. She couldn't have taken much more.

That night before dinner, while they were having drinks on the terrace Antoine made a startling proposal.

'I've been thinking this afternoon, Jean Adrien,' he said, serving them small glasses of sweet vermouth, 'about an idea that I've had for a long time. I wonder if you'd be interested in it?'

Jean Adrien settled back into his chair and crossed his legs. 'What idea?' he asked, sipping the amber liquid.

Antoine reflectively swirled the wine in his glass for a moment, then said, 'I'd like to expand the market for Château Villon wines, perhaps in America. Would you be interested in handling distribution at that end?'

Jean Adrien's eyebrows lifted. 'That's certainly something to think about.' He turned towards Camille. 'What do you think about it?'

Camille could see he was interested, and it didn't sound like a bad notion, although she didn't know why on earth Antoine would want to set up a business that would throw them together over the years. 'Certainly, more and more Americans are drinking fine wines, so the market is growing,' was all she said.

'I'm glad you think so,' Antoine said. 'I'm sorry I have to drive to Paris tomorrow or we'd have some time to go into the details. I'll be away a few days, as you know.'

'Don't worry,' smiled Jean Adrien. 'I don't think I'll let another twenty years go by before I come back.'

The discussion of the proposal grew avid over dinner. Neither man seemed to notice that Camille took no part in it.

Deep in the night, tossing and sighing in her bed, Camille realised that, despite the firmness of her resolve to leave, some small part of her still longed for Antoine's knock on the door, for the miracle that would bring him to her to tell her that he loved her. Was she wrong to wait for him to make the move? Should she be the one to knock at the door, to tell him how wrong he was about Edouard? The thought made her breath come fast.

No, she couldn't do it. That Deslandes pride, which had kept her father and grandfather apart for so long, was at work in her, too. If Antoine, with his characteristically implacable arrogance, could actually believe she was having an affair, then she wasn't going to crawl to him on her knees to convince him otherwise. Bleakly she stared into the blackness. Besides, he wouldn't believe her.

When at long last there was a glimmer of pink at the window, she bathed and dressed, then watched the early morning sun fill the sky. Sitting there alone, the loss of her grandfather welled up inside her again, and she realised that losing Antoine wouldn't be any less severe.

A knock on the connecting door broke her reverie and set her heart beating wildly.

'Camille, are you awake?'

'Yes, come in, Antoine.' She strove to keep her voice steady as she looked at the lean, handsome face that had come to mean so much to her.

His dark eyes fastened on hers. He looked haggard, as if he, too, had had trouble sleeping.

'I'll talk to Monsieur Motte about how best to go about the divorce,' he said stiffly. 'I have only one request, and that is that we wait a suitable time . . . six months, perhaps, before you leave. It will be best for me . . . and for you, as well, in your future relationship with . . .' He broke off the sentence. His cold eyes seemed to freeze her heart. 'As you now know, the French are more concerned than Americans with appearances.'

'Yes, of course.' She made her answer deliberately

ambiguous. She was leaving with her father in just two days, but she didn't want to argue about it.

Jean Adrien was shocked when she announced she was returning with him to America.

'But I had the impression from Antoine last night,' he said, clearly startled, 'that you were staying for another six months.'

'We changed our minds this morning,' she lied. Her father had taken a strong liking to Antoine, and she wouldn't put it past him to call Paris if he thought she was leaving unannounced.

'Oh,' he said, clearly a little puzzled. Then he smiled. 'I'll certainly enjoy the company, and we'll be glad to have you home.'

'Thanks, Dad,' she said steadily. 'I'd better go and organise my things.'

'But why, *madame*?' Joséphine asked wretchedly, as her eyes filled with tears and two red splotches appeared on her plain face.

'He doesn't love me, that's why,' said Camille, selecting some clothing to take with her. 'I don't quite know what to do with all these gowns and things,' she added, her voice gently but firmly changing the subject. 'I'm certainly not going to be wearing them in Yountville or St Helena. And I want you to have Henri put the jewels into the safe, please.'

Joséphine tentatively fingered the velvet box, and said mournfully, 'It won't be the same without you, *madame* . . . I don't know how I could even stay if . . . if . . .'

Camille calmly finished the sentence for her. 'If he marries someone like Mademoiselle Jusserand?'

'*Oui, madame*,' Joséphine admitted in a whisper.

Camille walked up to her and put a hand lightly on her arm. 'I'm going to miss you, too, Joséphine, and I don't want you to be unhappy. I've spoken to Madame Chevillot about you, and there's a fine position waiting there for you if you want it. All you need to do is send her a note.'

Joséphine smiled weakly in gratitude and dabbed at her eyes. *'Merci beaucoup, madame.'*

'Now,' said Camille firmly. 'The train leaves first thing tomorrow, and there's a lot to be done. I have to convince Rémi to keep pruning.'

Camille managed to maintain a calm, reasonably cheerful front as she said goodbye to Henri, Madame Gounod, Rémi, and the rest, but the façade crumbled steadily after she left Château Villon and the train brought them closer and closer to Paris and the flight home. Jean Adrien, sensitive to her misery, did not try to force her into conversation.

'Camille,' he said suddenly as they reached the outskirts of Paris, 'why don't we call Antoine's hotel? If he's in, perhaps he could join us for a farewell drink during our stay-over.'

'Absolutely not!' cried Camille. 'It would be awful, and entirely unnecessary . . .' She halted, anxiety etched in her face.

'Hey, calm down, *ma chérie,*' he said, clasping his daughter's hands, startled by her vehemence. 'It's all right, never mind. I just thought you two had parted friends.'

Camille was silent, not wanting to lie any more.

There was a long pause while he patted her hands. Then he spoke again. 'You love him terribly, don't you?'

'Not enough to give myself to him when I know he doesn't love me. I have too much pride.'

'Pride. Yes, the Deslandes pride . . . the Deslandes curse.'

The passion with which he said it surprised her.

'Yes,' she responded with grim humour, 'and look where it's all led.' Then, to comfort him she added: 'Grandfather was so happy that you discarded yours enough to come.'

'If it hadn't been for Bernie breaking a promise, I wouldn't have.'

The memory of her father saying something like that the morning of his arrival came back to her. 'What promise, Dad?'

'You know the old creation myth of Fouquet Vineyard?' he said. 'How Bernie poured his life's savings into it, and how he practically stole those cuttings from Château Villon?'

'Of course—what do you mean, myth?'

Jean Adrien chuckled.

'That old rascal didn't have a dime's savings— spent all his money as he earned it on his family—he seemed to have a million needy nephews in those days.'

'Then where did he get the money . . .' she stopped and laughed. 'Don't tell me—from Grandfather.'

'Right. When Bernie stormed in to quit and read my father the riot act, Father not only calmed him down, he managed to get him to go along with a plan he'd been hatching ever since he realised our breach was serious.'

'Knowing Grandfather, I suppose he was too proud to just ask you back, and he knew you were too proud to return.'

'Sounds silly now, doesn't it?' Jean Adrien looked sheepish. 'Anyway, he gave Bernie as much money as he thought he could get away with, without arousing my suspicions. And he made him take the vine cuttings. He also made Bernie swear he'd never tell. Well, after twenty years, Bernie decided it was time to tell.

Camille silently shook her head in amazement.

Jean Adrien looked steadily at his daughter. 'Now, are you sure you aren't making a foolish mistake—something you might regret the rest of your life—out of pride, too? Are you sure Antoine knows you love him?'

Camille sat gazing down at her lap. 'I don't know anything about anything right now, Dad. Someday, when I can talk about it,' she said ruefully, trying to smile, 'I'll tell you what went wrong . . . that is, if I can figure it out for myself.'

CHAPTER TEN

THE California sun was strong, and Camille was hot by the time she reached the oak-encircled glen on the hill above the Fouquet Vineyard. She spread out her towel and stripped down to her white bikini. Then, sitting down at the edge of the little pond, she put her feet into the cool water.

At her pleading one summer years ago, her father had diverted some water from a nearby stream to create a small pond in the glen. Over the years, Camille had experimented with native plants and flowers that required little attention, until she had turned the glen into a beautiful, quiet place of retreat to which she had fled when she needed to be alone. She never needed it more than now, she thought.

Absentmindedly, she trailed her fingers in the water, watching the ripples fade into stillness, and feeling the hot sun on her shoulders. Wishing the pond were deep enough for a dip, she had to be content with scooping up handfuls of cool water and splashing herself. Refreshed, she stretched out on the towel to sunbathe.

At first she watched a turkey vulture soaring effortlessly against the deep blue, but after a while a heat-induced lassitude stole over her, and she closed her eyes.

It had been three weeks since Camille had returned home, and the pain had still to diminish. She had yet to get in touch with a single friend, to go anywhere, to do anything that would start her picking up the pieces of her shattered self. Soon, she knew, she would have to begin living her life again and put the past where it belonged.

She had brought a book along, but it lay unopened on the grass, and without meaning to she let herself drift into the memories again . . . the lovely, exquisite memories that haunted her waking hours, and sometimes her sleeping hours as well.

Not a leaf rustled, not a bird chirped to disturb Camille's imagination as she pictured herself talking to Antoine, laughing, dancing—all the scenes etched against the haunting beauty of Château Villon and the warmth of her grandfather's affection. She lingered on the memory of the night of the storm when Antoine had held her in his arms so tenderly, and kissed her so seductively. The image of his face was so real she could almost reach out and touch it, almost caress that strong cheek, and trace the line of his lips with her fingertips . . .

Camille stirred, reluctantly opening her eyes to the bright, cloudless, blue sky. The turkey vulture's lazy circling had taken it far away, almost to the horizon. She smiled wryly; even a buzzard didn't find anything of interest in her. She sighed despondently as the last wisps of Antoine's face faded from her mind. Except for her memories of her grandfather, she wished the whole miserable year in France would disappear, and for good.

She turned over on her stomach and picked up the book, but it was no use. The daydreams returned. Half an hour later, having never turned a page, she abandoned the effort.

Bernie was rummaging in the refrigerator when

Camille came in by the back kitchen door. He looked at her searchingly, noting her slightly sunburnt complexion. His old face showed worry.

'Been out ruining your complexion again, I see,' he said, his voice reflecting his lifelong disapproval of idleness. 'I was just going to whip up an omelette for myself. Can I make you one?'

'Let me do it, Bernie, please?' she said, dropping her things on a kitchen chair. 'I forgot it's Mrs Green's day off. I should have put up a casserole this afternoon.'

'There's not much you're aware of these days,' he retorted gruffly, but his voice was full of concern. 'Walking around like a zombie . . . not eating half the time.'

'That bad?' she asked, as she met his anxious gaze. Then, not giving him a chance to answer, she added, 'I guess I've been wallowing in self-pity long enough to deserve a lecture.'

'Oh, we were going to give you another week to shape up or ship out,' he said, his eyes twinkling.

'I'll bet!' she said, planting an affectionate kiss on his cheek.

She sat him down with a glass of chenin blanc at the kitchen table.

'Where's Dad?' she asked, moving quickly and efficiently around the kitchen.

'Having dinner at Art Richards'.' Bernie's features lightened as he watched her move with her old energy.

'Art Richards? Who's that?' She sliced a couple of tomatoes in half and prepared them for frying with bread crumbs, garlic salt, and olive oil.

'IMBEC's head man on the West Coast. He

moved into one of those old mansions in St Helena. I
heard he's spending a fortune redoing it.' He looked
at her, his brown eyes sharp. 'I heard Jean Adrien
ask you to go along this morning, and you said no.'

'Oh . . .' Camille blushed as she chopped up some
thyme and marjoram for the omelette. 'I guess I
don't remember . . . I mustn't have been paying
much attention.'

Bernie snorted.

'Why didn't you go?' she asked suddenly, as an
unpleasant thought struck her. 'Weren't you invited?'

'Don't start getting upset about imaginary problems,' he said sternly. 'I was invited, too, and Jean
Adrien tried to get me to go, but I'm too old for such
things . . . dressing up in an uncomfortable suit,
putting on *une cravate* . . .'

Camille laughed. Bernie probably didn't wear a
tie often enough to know the English word. She
whipped the six eggs to frothiness in two separate
bowls, then divided the herbs and added them. Next
she popped an English muffin into the toaster.

'Jean Adrien enjoys it, though,' said Bernie, shaking his old head. 'Naturally enough. He takes to high
society like a duck to water.'

'I suppose he would, at that,' she agreed, grinning.

'Now that he's a major stockholder in IMBEC,
people seem to think he's hungry. He gets so many
dinner invitations he could eat three times a night if
he wanted to.' Bernie paused a moment. 'He'd be
having a fine time of it, too, if he weren't so worried
about you.'

'Well, he can stop worrying and so can you,' she
said firmly, as she stirred the first omelette in the

pan. 'It's funny, I guess I hadn't even given the inheritance a thought. Dad's suddenly an important person, isn't he?'

'He's not the only important person around here,' Bernie responded with pride. 'As soon as you start showing your face around the valley, you'll have more attention than you'll know what to do with, too. Especially male.'

'It sounds awful,' she retorted, folding a third of the omelette over on itself, then, with a flick of the wrist, expertly flipping it out on to a warmed plate. Quickly, she cooked the second and served the meal.

Bernie took a bite of the flavoursome, moist omelette and sighed appreciatively. 'Ah, *omelette aux fines herbes*—and perfect! At least you haven't forgotten how to cook.'

Camille ate some of hers and realised that for the first time in what seemed like ages she was hungry.

'It does taste good,' she said shyly.

Bernie happily watched her eat. 'No man's worth starving over.'

'True,' she said, smiling reluctantly.

'Well, that young idiot better stay out of my way when I'm back there visiting my family,' he said formidably, 'or I'll wring his neck like a plucked chicken's!'

'Oh, Bernie, you're a darling . . . but they'd lock you up for assault, and where would I be without you?'

The next morning, Camille resolutely assumed a cheerful expression and joined her father and Bernie for breakfast. Both men visibly relaxed when they saw her bright face.

'Good to see you looking so chipper, honey,' said Jean Adrien as they sat down.

Listening to the two discuss their plans for the day over bacon and eggs, she was amazed by the change in her father. It was startling to realise how unobservant she had been. To begin with, he wasn't wearing work clothes, but a suit—with *une cravate!*—and his conversation was about things like staff meetings and business luncheons, and the need to hire additional men because he would be tied up more and more in business affairs.

'Do you have any plans today, Camille?' Jean Adrien asked, turning to her.

'Yes, I'm going to tag along with Bernie and find out how he did without me all this time.'

Bernie snorted and said, in gruff affection, 'Get in my way is more like it. We're going to start harvesting the lower half today.'

After a busy morning of helping Bernie and watching the harvesting get underway, Camille slipped away to the glen after lunch. Although she was determined to act more maturely in the future, she didn't see any harm in retreating occasionally to be by herself. Besides, she realised a little forlornly, with two additional full-time workers and a housekeeper, she wasn't needed as much as in the old days.

Stretching out again on a towel next to the pond, she closed her eyes and savoured the warmth of the sun on her already tanned skin. The sound of buzzing insects and the chirp of sparrows deep in the bushes, hiding from the heat of the day, sounded softly in her ears.

Today, though, she was determined to drive Antoine out of her daydreams. Instead of the happy times, she ruthlessly forced herself to remember another train of images: Antoine kissing Eugénie in the garden, Antoine looking at her with hatred when he accused her of having an affair with Edouard, Antoine kissing her contemptuously that one last time . . .

There was someone in the glen; she felt it. Startled—no one ever intruded on her private place except by invitation—she opened her eyes. Antoine was standing there, between her and the sun, his form blindingly outlined in its light. She stared blankly. Was this a daydream within a daydream? She blinked in the brilliant sunlight and shaded her eyes with her hand. 'Antoine . . . ?'

'You little hellion! Haven't you caused me enough trouble without making me travel halfway around the world? And right at harvest time?' The sharpness of the tone jolted her back to reality.

'Antoine!' she gasped, sitting up. 'What are you doing here?'

He smiled grimly. 'What the devil are *you* doing here is a better question,' he said as his eyes took in her body, barely clothed in the brief bikini.

Blushing, she reached for her terrycloth cover-up, but Antoine grabbed it before she did.

'I don't know what you mean,' she said. 'This is my home, and will you please give me my cover-up!' Her voice trembled.

'No, I'm your husband and in the future I will look at you as much as I want. And no, this isn't your home. Your home is Château Villon.'

She stared up at him, transfixed. 'I'm sorry, Antoine, I just couldn't stay for six more months just to save appearances—'

'You might have considered what a fool I'd look like when I came home asking for you and my *servants*,' he flung the words at her, 'had to tell me you were gone!'

'I can't imagine that bothered you very long,' she scoffed icily, his tone stiffening her spine, 'once you realised you were free of me! You can even marry again sooner—this time to someone of your own choice! Someone like Eugénie Jusserand!' She rose to face him more levelly.

Antoine towered above her even when she stood. 'Oh, *certainement*,' he said in a harsh voice. 'The house servants would welcome a new mistress with open arms, not to mention the estate workers—who thought I had forced you to leave, and were so angry they almost went on strike. They would have too, if Rémi hadn't convinced them that you left of your own accord.'

'I'm sure all that will pass—'

'Yes?' Antoine said sharply. 'And what am I to do with the invitations I'm receiving from a great many important people demanding to meet the beautiful Madame de Breze, whose portrait was the hit of a major Parisian art exhibition? Eugénie would have a hard time passing as you.'

Camille was shocked into silence for a moment. 'The portrait . . .' she managed to stammer. 'I forgot all about—'

Antoine spread his long legs and put his hands on his hips. 'And if all that isn't enough to drive a man to drink, Rémi is having your section of the vineyard picked and crushed separately. The quantity is sufficient, and the quality of your grapes is so superior, he says that the new wine will win a *Grand Cru*.'

'Oh . . .' Then, with her face full of pain, she said hoarsely, 'I'm sorry I've caused you such trouble, but nothing you've said is reason enough for me to go back with you and continue that charade.'

Antoine stared back at her, his jaw set. Then a slow smile lit his features and his eyes softened. 'There is one more reason. I also love you very much, *ma petite*. I have for a long time now, but I've been guilty of a gross error of judgment about you . . . and Edouard. This time it won't be a charade.'

Camille's eyes widened in astonishment. 'You . . . you beast . . .' she sputtered. 'Making me think—'

Laughing, Antoine pulled her into his arms. As she struggled to escape he crushed her closer. 'Stop it or I'll turn you over my knee as I should have at the very first.'

His mouth sought hers and he kissed her so deeply and longingly that she not only stopped struggling, but entwined her arms tightly around his neck and strained against him, her own impassioned responses matching his.

His hands wandered urgently over her body, barely hampered by her swimsuit. '*Mon dieu*,' he said thickly. 'I've waited much too long for this. He pulled her down on the towel, breathing erratically. 'Far too long.'

'Not here, Antoine,' she gasped, the wonder of it all making her laugh and cry at the same time.

He was lying half over her, kissing her throat feverishly, his hands undoing her top. 'Why not?' he murmured. 'Bernard—who threatened my life with a pair of pruning shears, by the way—told me no one invades your garden.'

He tossed aside her top. Eyes closed, she felt a tide of ecstasy as his hands caressed her.

'How incredibly beautiful you are,' he whispered, looking down at her bare breasts, pearly white against the rest of her creamy, tanned skin. In another moment she felt his lean hard body, now divested of clothes, next to her. He swept her into his arms, and the warmth grew to an all-consuming fire. She was irrevocably lost as he possessed her, body and soul.

Later—much, much later—he lay on his side, propped up on one arm, looking down at her with a gentle and loving gaze.

'I don't recall hearing from your lips, *ma chérie*,' he said with amusement, idly chewing on a long stalk of grass, 'that you loved me.'

'I don't recall your letting me get my breath long enough to say anything,' she whispered, looking affectionately up at him. 'Besides, you should have been able to tell all along—it must have been written all over me in neon lights every time you came near.' She traced the outline of his lips, as she had in her daydream.

He kissed her fingers and grinned. 'I suppose I wasn't very good at reading your expressions. I plan to spend a great deal of time studying them now, though. I thought you hated me ever since . . . well, ever since the night you saw me kissing Eugénie. Then when you seemed to switch your affections so easily to Edouard, I'm afraid I despised you.' He paused, then added, 'At least I tried to.'

'Edouard was never more than a friend to me,' she said softly. 'But I didn't want to tell you that because I wanted to keep you at arm's length.'

'But why?' challenged Antoine, his brow furrowing.

Camille nestled closer against him. 'I was so afraid you wouldn't love me on your own, but that you'd pretend, if you thought it would affect the inheritance. I know how much you love Château Villon.'

'Then why didn't you tell me after Uncle Charles died? *Mon dieu*, Camille, you had three whole weeks!'

'You made me angry. I tried to tell you once that we weren't lovers and you didn't believe me . . . I was too proud to tell you again.'

'Ah . . . that dangerous Deslandes pride.' He smiled wryly. 'I guess I'd better tread more gently in the future. Life was intolerable with you, but it's been even worse since you left. Unfortunately, I seem to need you more than life itself. Camille, I could never go through losing you again.'

Camille reached up and pulled him down. Their mouths clung in a long, sweet kiss.

'You know you're torturing me with suspense, Antoine. How has this wonderful, beautiful, exquisite change come about?'

'The portrait, you silly goose. Edouard delivered it on our anniversary.'

'But it's been two weeks since then. Why didn't you call or come right away?'

He looked sheepish. 'I refused to see Edouard when he delivered it. Certainly, seeing it made me rethink what you'd been doing all those Tuesdays and Thursdays, but I still thought you loved him. I was insanely jealous.' For a second a fierce look came back into his eyes. 'If it had been a hundred years ago I would have had Edouard out on the duelling field. Fortunately, though, Edouard braved my anger and

kept coming back until he finally talked Henri into
letting him in. He bearded me in my den to set me
straight, and here I am.' He leaned down and kissed
her gently. 'I did misjudge you and Edouard both.'

'I'm so happy the painting was a success,' said
Camille. 'He'll be drenched with commissions.'

'He already is. Your portrait is magnificent! And
even though I was wrong about him, until I have you
firmly trapped by a child or two, I'm going to make
sure you have a chaperone around that man.'

She smiled shyly. 'You sure didn't waste any time
getting to work on that, did you?' she teased.

He shrugged. 'All Château Villon lacks *now* is a
new little heir tearing around the place. We'll name
him after your grandfather, of course.'

'I'm so deliriously happy, Antoine,' she said with
eyes softly glowing. 'I do love you with all my heart. I
just wish he knew,' she said, her voice faltering.

'Don't worry, *ma femme*, I'm sure he knows,' he
whispered, his lips claiming again what was his and
his alone.

Harlequin Announces...

Harlequin Superromance™
NEW

IMPROVED EXCELLENCE

Beginning with February releases (titles #150 to #153) each of the four Harlequin Superromances will be 308 pages long and have a regular retail price of $2.75 ($2.95 in Canada).

The new shortened Harlequin Superromance guarantees a faster-paced story filled with the same emotional intensity, character depth and plot complexity you have come to expect from Harlequin Superromance.

The tighter format will heighten drama and excitement, and that, combined with a strong well-written romance, will allow you to become more involved with the story from start to finish.

WATCH FOR A SPECIAL INTRODUCTORY PRICE ON HARLEQUIN SUPERROMANCE TITLES #150-#153 IN FEBRUARY

Available wherever paperback books are sold or through Harlequin Reader Service:

In the U.S.
P.O. Box 52040
Phoenix, AZ 85072-2040

In Canada
P.O. Box 2800, Postal Station A
5170 Yonge Street
Willowdale, Ontario M2N 6J3